A DARK NIGHT IN DERBY

Harvey Wood

A Dark Night in Derby

8.00pm Tuesday September 20th 1960

The streets were dark and slicked wet from the recent rain. The houses were terraced in long rows packed in along the narrow streets, quiet and empty at this time of the evening in autumn. Dark clouds scurried overhead in the stiff wind and the street lamps were throwing flickering reflections of yellow and white light from the puddles. Martin trudged along oblivious to all of it. Martin Baxter, a person who should be full of life and fun at his young age but instead he was a lonely young man just eighteen years old. His brown raincoat had seen better days and flapped about his legs in the cold wind as he walked. He kept his head down and his hands thrust deep in his pockets clutching at the few possessions he had with him. A handkerchief, a few boiled sweets, the key to the house where he lived with his parents and a few coppers was all there was.

He had walked these streets a thousand times before, keeping out of the way from home for as long as he could. His parents were all right some of the time he supposed but they weren't interested in him one bit, they never supported him, only shouted at him and chided him for the things he did no matter how small, good or bad. It had always been like that and he had become used to it and most of what was said he just shrugged off his back. They were always arguing about something, his father making the quarrels mostly. He was a big brute of a man who dominated his wife Mary and Martin. He was turning to fat now and had lost most of his hair; he hardly ever shaved or washed that well and had a rounded face that always seemed to have a sneer on it. His mother was no better really; she never had any time for him, never stuck up for him with his father or helped him really in any way. Martin wondered why they had given birth to him in the first place but then he imagined it had been a mistake just like the rest of his life was turning out to be. He had no brothers or sisters or any other family to turn to or if he did he didn't know about them, nothing was ever mentioned and he had never asked. Being an only child had meant a loneliness of sorts all his life although he had become accustomed to it over time and was actually quite happy with his own company. He had always found it hard to make and keep friends either so he lived in his own little world where he did what he could and virtually what he wanted, the lack of money being the only restrictive thing, which is what he knew he really had to sort out soon with a job of some description.

He lived in a working men's area of Derby, which some would say was the rough area of the town although there were many good people to be found there. Martin didn't really know any of them, not even his closest neighbours as most people just kept themselves to themselves and didn't get involved with others very much. He imagined he looked pretty rough at that moment though, what with his damp unkempt brown hair that needed a cut and kept on falling in his eyes and his scruffy clothes of corduroy trousers, white shirt that was in need of a wash and a thick green woollen jumper under his raincoat. His shoes could do with a clean and he could maybe do with a bath too but none of this really mattered, at least not to him. All he was interested in was carrying on and getting through yet another day. He had no thoughts of getting a girlfriend, after all who would have him, or doing well in a job, he just needed something to make him some money. The work he had already done were simple low paid jobs that he had no interest in nor gained any satisfaction from. His latest job had been packing sweets in a factory but he became bored of it and made too many mistakes now he was out of a job with no prospects. He lived on the pittance he got from the social security and the fact that he didn't pay board at home, well not very often, another thing that didn't go down very well with his parents especially his father who

5

was always on about him being lazy and that he should get a job and pay his way. At times when he was working Martin found he had to give most of his money to his father, more than he considered was fair but then he wasn't always in work so he supposed it evened out in the end.

Most evenings he would walk the streets just to be alone and not to be bothered by anyone. Alone he was and always had been, friends had come but quickly went again, preferring to be with more lively people and those who had a bit of money which Martin certainly did not have and he couldn't take them home, not to what they would find there. Apart from the fact that his parents could be in and would not be friendly to them there was also the issue of the state of the place. No one made an effort to keep it clean and it was untidy with items left anywhere. He kept his own room tidy enough though and as clean as he could but even so he doubted if the friends he did make would appreciate the effort.

Life at school had not been good for him. He didn't make many friends being quite a loner all his life. He had no real interests to join in with the other boys. He didn't like sports, he thought they were a waste of time although strangely he liked to run and keep fit when he was alone. Football was of no interest either although everyone he knew seemed to rave about it. Again he just couldn't see the fun of trying to kick a ball about past other boys into a net. The whole thing just seemed ludicrous, stating this to his friends was met with hostility so he stopped talking about it or anything else and just kept to himself as much as possible. His teachers noticed how he was and tried to get him to involve himself in various activities but to no avail and they gradually all gave up on him. Exams were a farce for him too as he never bothered to swot up on the things he ought to have but spent time studying things he found to be of interest and so he had left school with no qualifications whatsoever. Nature and all things of the outdoors was one of these things and he loved to be alone as far away from people as possible listening to the birds or trying to spot any animals he could. He could spend time just sitting looking around him at the trees, flowers, and insects, anything that presented itself and be at peace. He had an interest in English too and liked to write about the things he saw and did which he kept in notebooks in his room.

He thought that later on maybe he could find work that fitted into the things he liked but he hadn't found anything so far and without any qualifications it would be hard but still he hoped it would happen one day.

His favourite walk was through the Arboretum, a large park area close to his house, which had an entrance from his street. It had many tall mature trees on raised rolling banks of mown grass and well maintained flowerbeds. There was also an aviary where he would often stop to watch the birds in the array of pens. It was quite famous being Britain's first public park with a collection of many fine trees of different species. There were many flowerbeds along the pathways, which wound their way through the park, and in one area there was a bandstand, only used at the weekends and special occasions. Another part of the park he liked was the orangery, which was a long low building in red brick and faced with eight tall vaulted windows to let light into the area in which several exotic plants grew. He would often sit here, sometimes just to get out of the rain and it was usually quiet. A clock tower on the top gave him the time and a water tap a drink when he needed one. It was quite a narrow building and the back entrance opened out into a cul-de-sac, which then led on to Osmaston road, which was a main route into the town.

Outside of the park he was careful where he walked; a red light area was close by, not somewhere he wanted to be so he kept well away from that part of the town and walked the little used streets away from there and along the main roads that linked them.

As the evening drew on there would be less and less people around which pleased him as he could just be by himself. There were also some alleyways he would go through that linked the streets together and gave access to the back gardens of the houses; these were narrow with tall red brick walls to either side to separate the gardens. They were paved in blue brick that were often uneven due to their age and wear and they criss-crossed the narrow streets giving views of the backs of the houses as they were walked along. In the evenings Martin would see lights come on in upstairs rooms, mostly behind closed curtains and he wondered who was in them and what they were doing, more interesting things than he was he always thought.

He was very familiar with the area, the people who frequented it and the houses and shops that were there. There was a shop close by opposite the Arboretum entrance that he sometimes bought the odd item from, a drink or some sweets and on occasion other things such as a packet of biscuits anything to delay him going home for as long as possible. That was alright when he had money to spend of course. Tonight he had no money except for a little change and the shop was shut now anyway and he trudged on regardless. It was getting colder and he kept his head down as he walked. Going into an alleyway was a relief as the wind stopped, blocked by the houses and it was going down one of these that it happened. He wouldn't have seen it if he had just walked on up to the main road just a few yards further on but something made him turn into the alley as he often did change his mind on impulse. This one had a cross roads halfway along going down the back of the gardens of the houses in both streets to either side. He crossed over the junction and then stopped dead. The hairs on the back of his head came up and bristled as he paused motionless his mouth suddenly becoming very dry. Slowly and quietly he turned round and crept back to the junction, all his senses coming on alert as he listened and looked very carefully. He kept to the rough brick wall at his side and held onto it as if to make his actions that much smoother and quieter. Slowly he advanced back right up to the corner of the junction. Then after taking a deep breath he gradually moved so he could just see down the alley. Someone or something was there. Something that was not right, something that shouldn't be there and never had been there before in all the nights he had walked this way.

He looked down the alley breathing slowly and shallowly as if that would help him be invisible. Something was definitely there and moving. It was dark and he had to stare hard to try and make out what he was seeing. Then slowly it all began to make sense. There was a man, a big man in a dark coat, a trilby hat hiding most of his face and he was leaning over something lying on the ground, something rounded and... No, no it couldn't be, he could not believe it not until the man turned it slightly towards him and then he could see that it was a girl. She was lying on the ground her clothes all askew, he could see a flash of legs and then the man was bending over her again. Martin must have made a sound, a croak, a sigh or something because the man suddenly looked over to where he was. Martin froze not daring to move at all until the man looked back to the girl, so luckily he hadn't seen him in the dark. Martin breathed a sigh of relief and wondered what to do. The man was big and obviously older than him, how could he hope to overpower him even if he had the courage to try?

Then it was all too late, Martin watched spell bound as the man produced a knife and it seemed in slow motion that the girl raised an arm but too late as the knife went down and plunged into her again and again. Martin thought he was going to be sick, he could feel the bile rising in his throat. He could not help but make a noise as he tried to keep it down and that was when the man looked up again but this time he saw him, he now knew that Martin was there watching. The man rose to his feet and then he was coming towards him running fast. There was only one thing Martin could do, run, run as fast as he had ever run. His feet clunked down onto the uneven bricks that were the paving stones as he took off like a rabbit back the way he had come and out into the street. Quickly he ran off and as he did so he could hear the man coming up behind him his boots making even more noise on the pavement as he thundered on after him. He wasn't shouting at him he was just coming on which made it even more frightening.

Martin was in a panic. He had chosen these streets to walk along because they were quiet and no one much was ever about, now he wished that there was someone, anyone at all that he could turn to for help. He had to get away from the man to prevent him from catching him but how, then he thought that maybe the man did not know the area, or that maybe that he knew it better than him, he should do by now with the amount of time he had spent walking around. Now he started to use that knowledge to his advantage and he led the man off into another alleyway system and part way down he stooped low and squeezed under a fence where some boards had come loose into a garden, fortunately he was a slim boy, even undernourished some would say and he squeezed through easily enough but then just as he was through he felt his ankle caught in a vice like grip and the man's voice saying, 'Got you lad, now come back here.'

Martin was not going back, not of his own will anyway, he kicked and jerked his leg crying out, 'Get away, let me go.' But the man was strong and he hung on and began to haul Martin back through the gap. Tears came in Martin's eyes as he fought back, terrified that he would be killed as well if he were ever pulled through. He kicked again and looked for anything to hold onto to prevent his remorseless movement backwards. His leg was already through the gap and Martin realised the man was trying to grab his other leg. Desperately he kicked out again and he heard a satisfying howl of pain as his foot connected with something and then suddenly he was free. He struggled back through the gap, heaved himself up and ran on listening to the man's protests as he tried to climb the fence. Martin did not waste time looking round but ran on across the garden, through a narrow gap in another fence then across another garden and over a fence before he fell to the ground and then vaulted over a wall before making off along another alley into a street which he crossed before going back into the Arboretum where he knew there were plenty of places to hide.

He hurried on across grassy banks, between trees and through shrubberies. All this seemed to be working as the sound of the man behind him faded to nothing. Then checking behind him that he had lost him and that was not being seen he ducked down the narrow gap at the back of the aviary between the wooden boards and the outer brick wall of the park and pressed himself up against the boards and tried to control his breathing. Maybe, he thought he ought to have gone to a phone box and dialled 999 but then he hadn't really had the chance to do that. There weren't many of them around and it really would have taken too long to get to the nearest one and the man would have been on him.

For what seemed like ages he just stood there as his breathing slowed down and he could then hear again more clearly. There was no sound at all except for a little fluttering and tweeting from the birds in the aviary. He hoped those sounds would have hidden any noise he might have made and now he listened very carefully. It was getting really dark, there was no moon tonight, hidden behind the thick clouds scudding across the sky that promised yet more rain and it was difficult to see anything from the small space he was squeezed into. He looked both ways down along the aviary walls. If the man did know where he was then he would have to come at him from one side or the other and he would see him and could make off in the other direction. He was worried; he had just witnessed a murder, an actual murder. He could hardly believe it, here in a street very close to where he lived.

Time went on and there was no sign or sound of anyone approaching and Martin knew he couldn't stay there all night. He went over again in his mind of what he had witnessed. A man, bending over a girl with her clothes torn, a knife, her being stabbed. Then the awful thought came to him, what if she was still alive and lying there in the alleyway in agony? Martin didn't know but then the man had stabbed her more than once and then he had seen him and given chase. What should he do? Go to the police, yes that seemed to be the best idea, but then he had hardly seen him so how could he describe him? His hat had been pulled down low and there had been a scarf over the bottom part of his face, all that he had seen were his eyes which just looked like dark circles, hardly a description. Then it came to him. Whoever it was, he had left his knife behind, no doubt still buried in the girl; he had seen the man rise up without it. Surely he would want to go back for it now he had not been able to catch him, the only person who could identify him. There was only one thing for it, he would have to go back there, back to where it had happened, back to the girl and hopefully before the man got there so he could see if the girl was alive or dead and if she was still alive then maybe he could help somehow or at least get someone to call for an ambulance, but then what if she was dead and if the man returned while he was there then maybe he could get a better description of him of course. Could he do that without being caught? Well there was only one way to find out. Cautiously he eased himself out of the gap behind the aviary and looked around. There was no sign of him, in fact no sign of anyone and no sounds to alert him either so he slowly at first began to make his way back. He was frightened of what he would find and what might happen but there was no alternative, frightened or not he had to go back there and see what he could find out before going to the police.

All Martin's cunning began to come out as he made his way back by a circuitous route that would make it impossible for anyone to follow him without him knowing about it. It was slow work but he did it as quickly as he could and he had to keep looking around him and keep quiet as he worked his way back to where he knew the assault had taken place, however he knew all the shortcuts and it wouldn't take him too long to get back.

He wondered where the man was now. Was he still out looking for him or had he returned to the girl, in which case he may have already got the knife and he may be long gone. Martin couldn't bear that thought and hurried on, anxiously looking about him the whole time.

Then suddenly he was close, so close that he now had to take extreme care. What if the man was already there, or worse waiting for him to turn up so he could kill him as well? Martin's throat was very dry and his hands were shaking, why was it always the same, when he wanted someone they were never there for him? There was nothing he could do about it now, he had to carry on and hope for the best. He knew exactly where he was, the alley was just one street away and he knew he couldn't just walk in as he had before. Luckily with all the time he had spent around here he knew where all the alleys led, where the gardens were, the broken gates, the fences he could get through and he now used all that information to good effect by getting to the girl by a series of using that knowledge partly by going over one garden into the next. He wondered as he went whether to knock on someone's door for help but then by the time he had explained everything and when and if they had agreed to help him it could be too late and the man could have gone and the girl could have died or he could have taken his knife with him, the very proof that Martin would need together with as good a description as he could get. No, he had to carry on and get there first if possible. Slowly and carefully he proceeded and eventually he was there, well, close enough. He was in a garden behind a broken gate on the dark side of the alley and he could look through the gap where the gate didn't close properly to get a good view of where the girl was lying.

He now looked, and sure enough she was still there just a few yards down from where he was and there was no sign of the man, not yet anyway. The gate creaked as he tried to ease it open to get a better look and he had to stop then try again to get a big enough gap to squeeze through. The gate seemed to make enough noise to wake the whole neighbourhood but he kept on as quietly as he could. He could now see the girl better, she was not moving and Martin feared that she was indeed dead although he had to make sure and he pushed the gate again which complained with a loud creak as he squeezed himself through the gap and out into the alleyway.

Immediately he felt naked and vulnerable, in clear view if the man was here watching. He had come too far though to back down now so he quickly ran over to where she lay huddled on her side in a heap on the ground all his senses coming alert. She was wearing a short jacket that had been pulled off her right shoulder, her dress beneath was ripped open at the chest and it had ridden up high over her legs but, otherwise she was fully dressed and it appeared to him that she hadn't been attacked for any sexual reason. He bent down and tried to find a pulse but he wasn't sure how to do it but when he pulled at her shoulder to turn her over to look for a heartbeat it was then that he knew for sure that she was dead. She fell over onto her back, her face was a mask, a white grimace of pain etched all over it and she was cold, she was so cold. He knew instinctively that she was dead; there was no doubt about it to him at all. It was then that his hand brushed against the knife. It was embedded into her chest and there was blood, lots of blood all over her and the knife dark and sticky and getting onto his coat. Without thinking he tried to pull it out but it was stuck solid in her. He tried again with both hands but it was no use it was really fastened in, then he looked horrified at her blood, it was on him, on his hand, on his sleeve. He let go in shock and backed off slowly coming to his feet. He had to get away now. He hurried back behind the gate into the garden forcing it to close as much as it would and he leaned against the rough wood his heart all a flutter. What was he doing? What was happening? Things like this just did not happen to him.

He was shaking and his breath seemed to be shouting at anyone around it was so loud. He had to calm down, stay as calm as he could and be practical. He panicked as he came to his senses, the knife he had come for now had his fingerprints on it, that would be a great thing to hand in to the police. He looked at the blood on his clothes and on his hands, desperately he tried to wipe it off with his handkerchief but it wouldn't clean off. He thrust it back into his pocket, cleaning up would have to wait.

So what now? He stood indecisive, wondering what to do. Obviously he thought, the man had not come back yet for his knife, but then would he? Martin's mind was working overtim. With his own prints now also on the knife he was in a really bad situation.

* * *

Having caught the lad's leg Nathanial Armstrong thought he would end this easily but then he had caught a good kick on his wrist and had to let him go. He was horrified to find he had got away and was hurrying off away from him. Quickly Nathanial heaved himself over the fence and took off after him. It only took a few minutes for Nathanial to realise he was not going to catch him in a straight race so he stopped and found his way back to the street. It was fairly obvious the lad would have to travel by the streets at some point, all he had to do was watch out for him then get him. However as time went on it became obvious that wasn't going to happen that easily. He walked up and down the streets looking for him while keeping out of the way of anyone that happened along. He tried several streets in different directions and realised he was taking a lot of time and as he walked he was conscious of the fact he had left his knife in the girl and he would have to go back for it, he couldn't just leave it there for the police to find. He passed the entrance to the Arboretum and decided to take a look in. It was an obvious place for the boy to hide and he walked around carefully trying to keep out of view while checking that the boy was or wasn't there. After a while he gave up and returned to the street. So now he headed back carefully to where the girl was looking all around as he did so. As he got close he took extra care to check that no one saw him enter the alley when crept down to where the girl lay.

* * *

Martin's pulse was starting to slow down. It had been quiet in the alley for a couple of minutes and he wondered if indeed the man would return. Then he heard a noise, just a small sound, a pebble being moved, a scrape on the brick paving, someone was coming. Whoever it was he obviously was trying very hard to be quiet but Martin could then hear the sounds of footsteps approaching. He knew from his own experience what they sounded like when you tried not to make any noise. On and on they came, closer and closer to where he stood pressed up against the gate only a few inches away. He had to know who it was; maybe it was someone who could help him and not the man after all. Carefully he turned around silently and peered round the edge of the gate out into the alley his heart pounding again.

Someone was definitely there, a dark shape walking slowly but purposefully towards him, close, so close and then with a sudden shock he knew who it was. He had returned after all, the tall man in a black overcoat, he was here now approaching the gate right beside him. Martin quickly slid back into the garden behind the gate and as the man passed Martin could smell him, a musky smell and he could hear him breathing he was so close. Then after the man passed by he peered around the gate again. The man carried on and knelt down over the girl. Fascinated, Martin could not take his eyes off him.

Fortunately for Martin the light was very bad where he was hidden but the man's face was clear enough in the light that there was from the houses around. However, there was little to see. The man was still wearing a hat; the trilby and he had covered the bottom half of his face with the scarf. The only things Martin could see again were his eyes, which were like black circles that seemed to burn into Martin's face although he knew the man couldn't see him from where he was.

As he watched the man wrestled the knife from the girl's body, jerking it free with such force that the girl's body twitched and jerked before he then wiped it clean on her clothes and slipped it into a coat pocket. He searched in the girl's jacket pockets and rummaged inside them before pulling the girl's handbag off her shoulder, which he tucked under his coat and stood up. He looked up and down the alleyway slowly and carefully. His eyes swept across where Martin was hidden but he didn't see him. Instead he just turned and walked off back the way he had come walking past where Martin was hiding. Martin silently ducked back inside the garden again away from the gate, fearful that he would be discovered.

After a few seconds Martin returned to the gate and was frozen to it, his heart was beating like an express train and he could hardly breathe. Where was the man going now? Martin could only guess that it would be to his home. Slowly he prised himself away from the gate and looked out into the alley. The man had reached the end and was turning a corner out towards the next street. Martin did not think what he was doing but he ran as silently as he could down the alleyway after him. If he could follow him and find out where he lived then he could go to the police with that information too but first he had to follow him carefully so that he wouldn't be seen. That, he thought should not be too difficult. He had played the game with friends before but mostly on his own of following people, anyone, just to see if he could do it like in the movies without them knowing. Now he would see if those hours spent had been fruitful.

* * *

Julie West had been a model girl at school, always polite, always did her homework on time, never caused any bother to anyone. She had been a perfect student who kept out of trouble and always pleased her teachers. She worked hard and did well in her exams. She was certainly a pretty girl with her long blond hair and was always dressed nicely in clean fashionable clothes, all of which made her attractive to boys although mostly she wasn't interested. She was more interested in just enjoying herself with her friends who were mostly girls but also some boys who treated her like a friend and not as someone to try and get intimate with.

Her best friend was Sheila Hobbs who was in her class. They were both coming up to finishing school and soon would be looking for jobs. They would often meet up and go out together or just stay at one or the others house and play pop music on their record players and chat. Both girls got on really well almost like sisters as they liked to think of themselves, as they were both only child's. They did their hair together shared stories about boys at school and spent a lot of time together either going to the pictures, flirting with boys they met while out and those from school or generally just hanging out together. They had known each other practically all their lives and at one time had been neighbours but then Sheila's parents moved her away. Even so they were not far apart and could easily get to each other's house.

So it came as a bit of a surprise for Sheila to learn that Julie had been keeping a secret from her, which is something she had never done before.

Julie did have a secret, a very special secret that she wouldn't dare tell anyone about, not even Sheila. She had kept it for a little while and only mentioned it in her diary although she was very careful to keep this from her parents who she knew would definitely not approve. She really wanted to tell someone, it was hard to keep it to herself and Sheila would be the person she would tell if only she could bring herself to do it but she knew that she would be shocked and she was too embarrassed to talk about it quite apart from the fact that she had promised solemnly never to tell anyone.

It was coming up to Sheila's fifteenth birthday and she was going to have a party. Julie and Sheila had been meeting at Julies house for Sheila to talk about the arrangements for some days. They were in Julie's bedroom sitting on her bed. Sheila was sitting cross legged and had a notepad on which she was taking notes about what she was going to have to eat, what she was going to do on her party and who she was going to invite.

Sheila was a pretty girl almost as pretty as Julie. She had long straight brunette hair in contrast to Julie's natural blond locks and a more rounded face. In fact she was more rounded all over but not what would be called fat. She was bubbly and a very confident sort of girl, more so than Julie and had probably been instrumental in bringing Julie out of her shell somewhat. Both girls wore wide skirts with underskirts and often, white socks and flat shoes. Her eyes were a dark brown where Julies were a piercing blue and were both around the same height of just over five feet.

'It's going to be great Julie, there will be lots of food and drink and I am having my record player in the front room too so we can play what music we like and as loud as we like.'

'It sounds really good Sheila I can't wait, it will be fun.' Julie also couldn't wait to tell her of her news as she was bursting to tell someone, it was such a secret that she had to be careful what she said but in spite of herself she said, 'Actually I have some news too.'

'Oh really, good news I hope, what is it?' Sheila looked at her friend expectantly.

'Well,' Julie started, her head down almost sorry she had said anything then taking a deep breath she said, ' I have been seeing someone.'

'What a boy, who?' Sheila sat closer and put her note pad on the bed.

'Well not exactly a boy.'

'Oh Julie, who have you been seeing?'

'Don't look at me like that Sheila, there is nothing going on, it's not like that.'

'Oh,' Sheila said disappointed, 'Well what then?'

'It's someone I met a while ago and he has been very good to me, he gives me little jobs to do and he pays me.'

'Wow, that does sound good, I wish someone would pay me to do little jobs,' Sheila said then stopped, 'Er what kind of jobs Julie?' Sheila sat back and looked at her friend.

'Don't be silly Sheila, I mean work, well sort of. There is nothing between us I can assure you.' She smiled as the thought seemed funny to her, 'They are just little jobs that's all.'

'Just little jobs, you can't leave it like that now, tell me more?' Sheila shuffled closer up to Julie.

'I can't really say much more, it has to be a secret, at least for a little while longer. I'm sorry I shouldn't have said anything.' Julie suddenly pulled away, 'You won't say anything to anyone will you?' Julie said concerned looking at her friend.

'No of course not silly, not if you don't want me to.' Sheila was surprised and intrigued by her friend's news and actions. It all sounds very mysterious though you must tell me properly just as soon as you can. I must say, it sounds quite a secret, you dark horse Julie. I just hope you are being careful that's all.'

'Yes of course I am and you will be the very first person I will tell but for now let's get on with your party arrangements.'

Sheila stopped asking, but promised herself to keep on until she knew what the secret was just as soon as she could.

10.00pm Tuesday September 20th 1960

When Martin reached the junction in the alley he stopped and dropped down low before looking round the corner wall. He knew that anyone looking back would not expect to have a head appear at ground level. However, the alley was empty, the man had gone. Quickly Martin got to his feet and hurried along to the street where he peered out carefully in both directions. The street was empty. There was no one to see. At this time of night it was normally like this, at least until later when the pubs started throwing people out.

'Which way did he go?' Martin thought desperately, and he imagined the street layout here. He knew every street and alleyway in the whole, every unlocked gate, gaps in fences, even the layout of most of the gardens having explored them all while keeping away home and the grief he knew he would find there. It wasn't mum he worried about, she really wasn't so bad, at least she didn't shout too much but when dad was in then there was always trouble. He was a bully and a lout, selfish and always with a chip on his shoulder about something.

Racking his brains he thought through where the streets would lead and dismissed going right as that went into an area of virtually all old people, some of them he knew though not to talk to before the street ended up at the main Normanton Road. So he turned left and hurried off to the corner of the street. As he got there he peered round the corner and there he was, well had been, he only just caught a glimpse of him as he walked around the next corner onto the main road. Martin was at that corner in seconds but now he had to be more careful, the main road went on for a long way and it was pretty much open all the way although Martin knew if he kept to the right hand side, the opposite of where the man was walking then there were places that he could nip into if he needed to.

Keeping as calm as he could he walked on keeping a good distance between himself and the man who was now walking off at a good pace. Now there were occasional other pedestrians which Martin was thankful for, some were probably going or coming from work, others maybe going home from the pictures which would have closed just a short while ago, either way it meant he wasn't alone and not quite so conspicuous.

Then ahead, the man crossed the road glancing his way as he did so and started walking down another side street. Now that he was out of sight Martin ran over and carefully turned into the street and slowed down immediately. The man had stopped. Martin cursed himself for being so careless, he should have stopped as he had before and peered around before stumbling in. He couldn't see what the man was doing but he was facing away from Martin luckily and fumbling in his pockets. Martin wondered if the knife had cut through his pocket or become lodged somehow and he was trying to free it. Whatever it was he started walking again much to Martin's relief and it didn't seem as though he had been spotted.

Martin followed on, more carefully now after that shock. The man made several more turns and as they progressed Martin began to guess where he was heading. The whole time they were walking roughly south away from the town. There was a housing Estate to the left which was a maze of houses, it would be easy to follow him there but instead the man suddenly turned off into another alley that then went over a long bridge over the railway lines. This was now very difficult for Martin. The bridge was very long and made of metal. There was a long staircase to take it up over the tracks at either side and it would be impossible to cross it silently and as there was no one else around there was nothing else for it but for Martin to stop and wait at the staircase until the man had crossed over. He would not be able to watch him either because as soon as the man got to the top of the steps he would be out of sight. All he could do was wait and guess at how long it would take the man to cross over completely and down the other side before going after him. He was worried now that he might lose him, as this would put him some way behind. There was nothing for it though but to wait which Martin did fretfully.

Once he was sure the man must have crossed to the other side Martin started up the steps and at the top looked down the length of the bridge wondering if he had given him enough time. For once he was happy that he could not see his quarry and he hurried along as quietly as he could although every step sounded like a church bell to him.

At the end he hurried down the other steps and out onto a dirt track, which led to another busy road. There was no sign of the man at all and anxiously Martin hurried along to the main road. There he stopped and looked both ways. The man was nowhere to be seen, he had lost him. The bitter disappointment rankled Martin and he stamped along to the left having decided each way was as good as the other. Both ways led to other main roads with lots of houses and the man could be going to any one of them. It had been a difficult choice but he thought he might as well take this route, which would take him nearer to home if indeed he had lost him.

What was he up to now? Had the man crossed the bridge on purpose so he could tell if anyone was following him? There was no way Martin could know, with his hands in his pockets he carried on purposefully towards the main road. He couldn't go to the police now and if he did they would think that it had been him who had killed the girl, after all he had her blood on his clothes and maybe some of his finger prints on the knife if they ever found it although the way the man had pulled it free of the girl's body he doubted it but then he couldn't rule it out. At the very least he would have to get rid of his raincoat and get changed which would mean going home before he did anything else. After all he had done he now had no idea what the man looked like or where he was going to which hopefully would have been his home. Just his luck he cursed walking on.

The wind cut into him remorselessly while occasionally there was another shower to endure. Despondently Martin cursed his luck again as he turned into the main road and set off in the direction of home after having looked carefully at the next junction to see if he could see the man. There were more people around now that the pubs were closing but Martin paid no mind to them, as he was full of his own thoughts. Ahead of him a few men were walking along and as Martin passed two of them he looked at the man in front of him. He was only a few paces away and Martin suddenly realised who it was, it was him! It had to be; Martin had seen enough of his back now to know it was him. Where had he been? Martin could only assume that he had taken a circuitous route to ensure he wasn't being followed and somehow with luck Martin had managed to get behind him again. He smiled and slowed right down to allow a distance to open up between them. This time he wasn't going to lose him.

After some time the man turned into another side street and Martin waited at the corner until he had walked a good way down it. Then true to Martin's luck the man stopped and looked around. As he did so Martin ducked back around the corner then after a few moments he looked back down the street again. The man was letting himself into a house. Once he was inside Martin walked down the street to get the house number. The houses were mainly terraced buildings but there were a few palisaded in the street with very short front gardens, not really gardens just eight feet of bricks up to the front door, some with a privet hedge and it was to one of these that the man had gone into. Martin reached the house and kept on walking, noting the number twenty three on the door as he went past. Twenty three Winston Street, he would remember that.

The street was a dead end. It finished by going out onto fields and just a few yards further away was the canal which wound its way from the town centre through the fields behind the houses, beyond that open fields stretched away where some horses grazed under a group of trees. At the end of the street Martin took the risk of doubling back on the other side to try and see anything else of interest. There was a light on upstairs but the curtains were all drawn and the house looked just as drab as all the others in the street. The curtains looked dirty and the house generally uncared for including the tiny front garden. None of this mattered, Martin now knew where the man lived and it was just a question now of what to do next?

* * *

Sheila's party was a great success, she had invited friends that her and Julie knew at school as well as family members and they had a laugh playing pop records from the charts and singing along. Her parents had laid some food and drinks out for them all in the kitchen and there were balloons and streamers all around. Sheila's other friends Susan and Samantha were there with two boys, Malcolm and Steven and a few other friends as well as a few of the younger family members. The older members, aunts and uncles mainly stayed in the back room where her parents were, away from the noisy pop music that they didn't approve of. Sheila and her friends were all in the front room. They all got on well and were having a great time, telling jokes, playing silly games and listening to music, rather loud her parents thought. There was plenty of food and soft drinks available and they all were enjoying themselves.

Although it was quite busy Sheila found time to chat to Julie on the landing outside the bathroom at one point.

'Love those shoes Julie, are they new? ' She asked.

Julie looked sheepish before answering, 'Yes they are, then quickly tried to change the subject.

'I'd love a pair of red shoes like those, I must ask Mum for some.' Sheila persisted.

'Sheila, I will have to leave in a little while.' Julie said stopping Sheila.

'Why Julie? You have been very quiet all evening I was going to ask you what was on your mind only with everyone here I couldn't.'

Julie stopped her and took her hand, 'I'm sorry, it's just, well you know I told you about someone I was seeing?'

'Yes I remember, and you were very secretive about him. It's not like us to have secrets Julie you really must tell me all about it and soon.'

'Sheila, I will, I'm going to meet him tonight and tell him it's over, and that I don't want to work for him anymore and then once it's all done with

I will tell you all about it, I promise.'

'Oh Julie I don't know what has been going on but I feel pleased that you are doing that. I can't it wait until tomorrow to find out but the party will go on for a while yet can't you stay just a little bit longer?'

'No I can't, not really,' Seeing her friends expression she carried on, 'Well I suppose I can stay for a little while but then I will have to go, I need to see him tonight and get it over with.'

'This is a bit sudden though isn't it? It was only recently you told me about him. You are not worried about going to see him are you, would you like me to come with you?' Sheila was suddenly concerned.

'No, no it's fine I can manage on my own thanks, and I will tell you all about it tomorrow, things will be better then. I have just changed my mind about him that's all.'

'All right, well you take care, now let's enjoy the time we have before you have to go.' Giggling, Sheila led the way back downstairs.

* * *

Josephine Foster sat in the dark of her room listening carefully for any sounds. There were the usual noises from the other young people in the home, the occasional shouting, radios blaring out and the odd scuffle but it wasn't those noises she was listening for. It was the quiet sounds she strained to hear, the sound of someone walking on a carpet in the hallway. She had been in this care home for only a short time, just a few weeks in fact and already she felt she needed to get out of it. She had been shuffled from one home to the next after her parents had both died in a car crash and left her alone with no one else to look after her when she was only six years old. Now she was eighteen years old and she should have been able to get a place of her own and look after herself but it hadn't worked out that way what with one thing and another so here she was with her few possessions, curled up on the bed fully dressed late at night in a white tee shirt, warm red jumper, short fake black leather jacket, dark blue trousers and serviceable shoes all ready to go. She was quite a pretty girl, with an oval face and a generous smile; she had bright green eyes and natural blond hair that flowed in curls down to her shoulders. She also had a shapely figure, which she often tried to hide especially from boys although it never seemed to work because they liked to tease her. This was probably to explain why she was in the position she now was with Mr Henderson. She had never really got on with boys although there had been a couple she had liked but never had the chance to get to know. Mostly they just mocked her or wanted more than she wanted to give when she was with them. Now she just avoided them and dressed in ways to not show her figure and prevent them getting interested in her which worked pretty well.

Her social worker had been very good with her and had done the best she could to make things right for her but Josephine was not happy. Sure the place was reasonable enough and the other teenagers here were not bad to get on with. She had quite a nice room with its new white wardrobe and chest of drawers, a comfy bed and a table and chair all kept very clean. There was a shared bathroom down the hall, her clothes were washed and she was well looked after. The food was fine too but there was one person who made it all turn sour. One of the child care workers, he looked and seemed alright and had talked to her in a friendly manner when she had first arrived but as the days went on she could sense that there was something wrong, something she wanted to shy away from. He just didn't seem right more and more with the way he looked at her and the things he said. She had heard stories before in the homes about the men who worked there and she didn't want anything to happen to her. She had even mentioned this to her social worker hoping she would help her but she had seemed shocked to hear it and was unbelieving.

'Mister Henderson, no surely not, Josephine you have got him all wrong, he is one of the nicest people here.' Is what her social worker had replied when Josephine had expressed her doubts. 'Just try and get on with him, I am sure he is only trying to help you.'

So that was that, on one understood the situation she was in with him, she was on her own as usual, no one else at the home would help her and it was hard to keep away from him as well which made her feel really uncomfortable.

He had asked about if she had a boyfriend, what she intended to do with her life and had always sat just too close to her with that smarmy smile. Something definitely wasn't right about him and Josephine was not going to let him get any nearer to her, no way.

Mr Henderson was middle aged, in his late forties Josephine imagined. He was quite a big man with a paunch and always wore the same tweed jacket and a pullover with an open necked shirt, which put him apart from the others there who always dressed a lot smarter. He had a shock of light brown hair and a rounded face which always gave the impression that he was smiling whatever the situation. Josephine had been put with him for him to help her adjust to the new home and to assist her with her studies and anything else she needed. He had seemed ok at first although Josephine could feel his eyes on her, which made her want to shrink away. She always made sure she wore trousers and a baggy jumper whenever she knew she would have to see him.

Mr Henderson knew he was good at his job and indeed did do his best for those put into his charge. The only thing was that he had this penchant for pretty girls of which category Josephine fitted perfectly. He was pleased to help her where he could and also liked being with her but he was also a bit of a chancer and Josephine had heard innuendos and comments from the other girls about him but nothing really concrete and as she didn't get on with the other girls there she didn't really have the opportunities to discuss it so she just kept it to herself.

Josephine knew she was not going to get anywhere with her social worker about him and she stopped trying. She had a definite feeling that this man was not what he seemed and when that very morning he had suggested that he could help her with her studies that evening as she was trying to get qualified in care working so that she could maybe help others as she grew up her doubts deepened. She thought this could have been done during the day but he had arrived at her room earlier that evening when his shift had ended, which had seemed odd. She had reluctantly let him in to her room but all he seemed to want to do was look at her and talk about other things, such as what she was doing, who she was seeing. After a few minutes she feigned a bad headache and managed with difficulty to get him to leave as quickly as she could and now she sat wondering if or when he would come back. He had said he would call and check up on her again later so she expected he would. There was no lock on the door so she had wedged a chair under the handle just in case and she had packed her rucksack with all her things. For a while now she had kept a rucksack filled with virtually all her possessions such as they were as she always felt that she might have to leave anywhere quickly. It now sat beside her on the bed. It was a small room, with just enough space to walk around the bed to get to the wardrobe and the other furniture.

She was fortunate in that the only window in her room opened just far enough for her to squeeze through, there were no bars on the window which she had experienced before in some homes, this one opened a little way then stopped on a hinged bracket which she had managed to prise off with a borrowed knife from the dining room which she had kept and now it opened just wide enough to allow her to get through. So there she sat, wondering and waiting. Time went on and she began to think that maybe her fears were unfounded after all and she relaxed back and laid back on the bed her eyes feeling very heavy.

Just a few minutes later she suddenly came to attention and wide awake, what was that? Could she hear him? Some sound had alerted her. It could be anyone she argued with herself. People did move around at night. Then after a few seconds she watched enthralled as the handle to her door was pushed down from the outside. She could hear someone push against the door and a grunt of surprise and then her name being called softly and that was enough for her. She bounded off the bed grabbing her rucksack, quickly pulled the window as wide open as it would go for which she thanked her lucky stars was on the ground floor and threw her rucksack out. Then she squeezed through the narrow gap just as she heard him calling out to her to open the door. The gap was a tight fit and the top of her trousers snagged on the catch. Cursing she struggled hard to free them but they were stuck fast. Crying with desperation, she eased back slightly and then pushed her way through again pulling at her waistband in an effort to free herself. In doing so her trousers ripped but that gave her the space she needed and the next thing she knew she was tumbling out onto the lawn below the window. She didn't know if he had heard her or not but all she wanted to do now was run, run as fast and as far away as she possibly could. The lawn went on for a way up to the metal fence, which went all the way around the home. Josephine was aware of this and knew that the gates would be closed and locked at this time of night. However she knew where there was a gap in the fence at one corner. She had watched foxes coming in and out of it and it was there she ran to now. The gap was not very big but then fortunately she wasn't either. She pushed her rucksack through and with a struggle she managed to squeeze after it and out onto the street. Then she was up and away slipping the rucksack onto her back as she ran across the street and round the first corner out of sight of the home.

When Mr Henderson found the door wouldn't open he panicked. What was she doing securing the door? Her had to find out and with difficulty and as quietly as he could he forced the door open pushing the chair into the room.

Finding her gone and the window open the ran into the room to have a look and was just able to see a dark shape disappear around the building.

He left the room again quickly and closed the door having repositioned the chair and hurried off hoping not to be noticed back to his office his mind racing.

11.15pm Tuesday September 20th 1960

The dilemma Martin now had was whether to go straight to the police or to go home and change first? In the end he decided of course that he had to go home first and get some fresh clothes just in case things went wrong for him and the police did think that he had carried out the murder and in any case it didn't look like the man was going to go anywhere in the time it would take him to get changed and get to the police station and for them to come and arrest him, provided they acted quickly enough of course.

He was now some way from home and had a long slog to get back, back to the palisaded house he lived in just outside of the town centre.

The street was long and was mostly palisaded with some terraced as well with the Arboretum frontage taking a quite a few yards of the street. The entrance to the Arboretum was through elegant iron gates, which then ran on as high railings to either side of the gates, which altogether gave the street more of an upmarket feel. It was a reasonable area to live in really, better than a lot of others close by anyway. The houses were very large inside with high ceilings and long corridors with cellars and attics. They must have been very grand in their heydays but his was not grand at all, the opposite in fact. Being a rented house his parents had not bothered doing anything to it at all. The wallpapers were all old and faded, the paintwork shabby and yellowed. It was a cold house in winter particularly with only one coal fire for warmth in the living room. The furniture was old and battered, the sofa and chairs were well worn and everywhere was untidy. Nobody ever took the time to tidy up or dust and Martin doubted if anything had ever been polished. It was however home to him and he did his best with his own room, which thankfully his parents never bothered to enter, except only on rare occasions when there was a need to.

Eventually he arrived home, tired, hungry and thirsty. He had already been out for a while before his adventure had begun and now he was feeling the stress of it all as well as the weariness. Opening the front door to his home he walked into the hall listening hard to try and discover what his parents were doing, if indeed they were still up and not gone to bed. He could hear the radio on in the living room so one of them was up at least. He poked his head around the door and found his mum sitting there reading.

'Hi mum,' He called keeping most of his body in the hall.

'You're back are you?' Is all she said hardly lifting her head from the book she was reading.

'Just going to get something to eat.' Martin said. His mother just nodded so Martin closed the door and went to the kitchen. He took his coat off as he did so and folded it inside out ready to hide away and put it over a chair ready to take up to his room. Checking the kitchen cupboards and the thrawl in the back room did not reveal very much.

The kitchen generally was dirty; there were pots in the sink, a dirty tea towel hanging by a hook on the sink unit. The cupboards and floor could do with a clean. The cooker had grease on it from weeks ago and all the pots and pans had seen better days. Mary just couldn't be bothered to do anything and just got on with things. Martin looked around, there was some bread, a few potatoes left over from dinner in the pan and some cheese. Martin made himself a cup of tea and ate what there was. He then sat there thinking. Should he tell his parents what had happened? After a little deliberation he thought not to, they would only talk him out of going to the police not wanting any trouble to come to them, especially his father with the things he got up to and they wouldn't be worried about what had happened to the girl at all so he stood up, washed the pots he had used, picked up his coat and went up to his room.

He had always cleaned up after himself from an early age, his parents didn't seem to bother what a state the house was in which had made it harder for Martin to invite any friends' home. Now he always washed most of his own clothes and led a life quite distant from his parents. One day he would have to move out but with no money and no prospects that was going to be difficult, for now he just went from day to day, looking for work when and where he could always hoping to save a few pounds to do something with.

He felt a bit better in the safety of his room. It was quite large really as most rooms were in these old houses. There was lino around the edge of the floor and a large carpet in the middle. He had a bed by the window wall with a small table beside it and he went immediately to the old varnished wooden wardrobe on the opposite wall where he kept his clothes, there were some old suitcases and various boxes in there as well where he kept his things. He took a hanger off the rail, put his raincoat on it and stashed it at the far end of the wardrobe where it would stay until he could get around to washing the blood off it. He checked his bloodied hanky was still in a pocket in the raincoat to wait until later too. The rest of the room consisted of a desk and chair and that was all. He chose a black zip up jacket, a pair of clean dark blue jeans and a dark brown cap from his wardrobe then turned to go out. He looked down at his bed wishing he could just lie down and go to sleep and let the events of the evening just wash away. For a few moments he hesitated, would it really be too bad to have just a few hours sleep then go to the police? He sat on the edge of the bed for a few moments then decided it would be best to go now while it was still fresh, if he lay down that would be it and it would be morning before he woke up. So he crept back down the stairs quietly so as not to alert his mother and went out into the street again. He would not be missed now until the morning at least so he had plenty of time.

He wondered what his father would think of him if the police arrived at his house at some time after he had been to see them? Not a lot, in fact both his parents would be very negative about it. His father had never liked the police, no doubt partly because of them catching him on frequent occasions for petty theft and a couple of occasions of GBH. He would sometimes come home with items he had 'found' or so he said, some of which he sold on and some he kept. Jim mostly had work, which changed frequently, generally labouring jobs and sometimes factory work, anything really, that he could pick up but still carried on with his nefarious activities.

He had been lucky to only have served a short term in prison for GBH and received a couple of cautions for various indiscretions. Not that any of this had really bothered him, he was the sort of man who could just shrug it off his shoulders and carry on. Prison only helped him to make new contacts and get more useful information. Jim was a big burly man, hard and strong, well able to take care of himself and cause trouble for others if it came to it. He didn't care about anyone else even his wife and son so long as he was all right that was all that mattered. He had put weight on recently and now spent a lot of his time just slobbing around the house moaning on all the time about anything and everything. He hardly ever bothered to shave and always had stubble on his face. Often he would lash out with a fist or a boot if he became angry or frustrated about something. Martin had learned to dodge out of the way on most occasions; his mother would try too but didn't always succeed. Having lost his last job in suspicious circumstances he was now doing occasional labouring work with a friends building business and taking the odd thing when and where he could to sell on.

Martin's mother, Mary was quite a hard person too, never having got anything easy she became involved with Jim when she was young, too young to marry her parents had said but marry she did and all had been fine for a while and she had given birth to Martin who had been conceived after a drunken night out. Now she had gotten used to Jim and his moods and even agreed with him on many occasions including some of his thefts and ill gotten gains. She had settled into her life and she just got on with it taking her pleasures when she could which was mostly reading, watching TV and smoking while keeping herself to herself always being secretly pleased whenever Jim was out of the house or in prison. At these times she could do just as she wanted. In the early days she used to meet up with her friends and go out to a club or a pub for an evening. Now that had all stopped as Jim became unhappy with her going out, especially without him and it wasn't worth the trouble going up against him. Martin was dreading the police turning up at the house, that would not go down very well at all he thought and he would not want to be there if and when it happened so it was with much trepidation that Martin carried on towards the police station.

12.15am Tuesday September 21st 1960

The police station was in the middle of the town so fortunately it wasn't that far to walk. At this time of night the streets were virtually deserted. The only people about were night workers and they had no interest in Martin as he trudged along keeping in the shadows to the building side of the pavements. It was a dark night, there was still no moon and dark rain clouds loomed across the sky allowing some rain to fall on frequent occasions. Martin had to stop once and take shelter in a doorway then hurried out again once the worst had passed. He was getting cold and wet and he hurried his pace to get to the police station.

Eventually he arrived and pushed his way through the double doors into the reception area, which was dimly lit by two yellowing light bulbs in white shades. The cream floor tiles had been freshly mopped and were slippy. It was a dismal place with its light green painted plain walls and a couple of plain straight backed chairs by one wall. There was a dark green painted counter ahead that filled the width of the end wall, it had a telephone and some paperwork on it but there was no sign of any police officers. Shaking his cap and coat to get most of the rainwater off them he went to the desk and rang a bell that was sitting there and waited, and waited. He supposed that at this time of night it would be quiet but surely there must be someone about. He rang the bell again and within a few seconds the desk officer entered from a door to his left behind the counter.

'Yes young man, what can I do for you?' The policeman asked. He was taller than Martin and broad, He had grey hair, what was left of it that surrounded his baldpate, with pink cheeks and a white moustache. Martin smiled as he thought he looked just like the typical policeman he had seen in books as he leaned on the counter looking intently down at Martin.

Martin then suddenly he found it hard to form the words. All the way down here he had been thinking over what he would say and practising it but now that he was here he stammered, 'I, I, er, that is...'

'Come on lad, spit it out.' The policeman said.

'I want to report a murder!' Martin finally said in a rush.

The policeman stared at him closely, 'Do you now.' He looked uncertain and glanced around to see if there was anyone else around that could help him but he was on his own. 'Right, well let's have some details shall we, name?' He asked.

'I don't know her name.' Was Martins feeble answer.

The policeman leaned over the counter towards him, 'Are you having me on?' He asked in a sharp voice.

Martin suddenly realised what he meant and blushed as he said, 'No, no I'm not, of course, my name, it's Martin Baxter.

The policeman wrote it on his pad then asked, 'Tell me about this murder then?'

'It's a girl she has been knifed, I saw who did it and followed him to his house.' It came out in an excited rush.

The policeman stopped writing, put his pen down and took another long hard look at Martin, 'Really! That was very clever of you. Well you had better come in lad.' He said and walked through the side door and out through another door into the reception area. 'Come with me'. He said beckoning to Martin.

Martin followed him through the door and on into the office area behind the counter. Here there were desks covered in paperwork and a few with telephones on, which were all deserted except one. The policeman pulled a chair out at an empty desk and beckoned to Martin to sit on one of the chairs opposite him. Then he called across to where a man was sitting at the back in plain clothes writing, 'Sir I think you had better come and hear this.' Grateful that he was there to help him.

The other man sighed, wrote a couple more words before looking up then he slowly rose unfolding his long legs he walked over and took a seat opposite Martin beside the officer, 'What have we got then?' He asked.

'This boy has come to report a murder, haven't you lad?' The policeman directed at Martin.

The other man looked at him surprised and said, 'I am Detective Chief Inspector Leonard Johnson. Tell me what you know? Sergeant, make notes.' He then sat watching Martin carefully while the sergeant went and sat at the next desk and pulled a pen and paper towards him.

'Take your time, just tell me exactly what happened.'

Martin slowly explained who he was, where he lived and about him seeing the girl, where she was and about her being stabbed and about the man and how he had seen him and chased after him and then how Martin had been able to go back to the crime scene and then follow the murderer home.

The detective listened very carefully only stopping him occasionally to explain more about certain points then he said, 'Get someone over there now sergeant!' DCI Johnson demanded of the policeman who then hurried off.

'That's quite a tale Martin. You have more explaining to do yet, 'Johnson said sitting back in his chair, 'Like why you went back there? Why you didn't come to us straight away.'

'I wanted to go back to see if she was still alive, there was no time to get to you, there wasn't any policemen around, no phone box close enough and no one else who could have helped me and then I saw my chance to follow him. If I hadn't I wouldn't have been able to tell you now where he lives.' Martin hurriedly explained not wanting to tell him about the blood on his clothes.

The detective didn't answer that but brushed his greying hair from his face and asked if he would like a cup of tea and explained that he would have to wait here while his story was being checked out.

He was taken to another room by yet another policeman, given a drink and left there. It seemed like a lifetime before another person, a sergeant came in to see him.

Looking very sombre the sergeant sat down beside him and said, 'I am Sergeant Wilson and I would like you to make a full formal statement.' He placed a report pad in front of Martin and a pen.

'But I have already told the other officer,' Martin protested.

'So now tell us again, this time write it all down yourself and leave nothing out. Start from the very beginning.'

Martin resignedly picked up the pen and thought for a few moments before starting to write.

As soon as he put the pen down Sergeant Wilson took the report from him and left the room. As he did so the officer entered who had brought him to the room and asked him if he needed anything.

'Another cup of tea would be nice please and some biscuits if you have any, are you going to tell my parents about this?'

The officer said that they probably would in due course, smiled apologetically and went off to get him another cup of tea and some biscuits. Martin frowned and wondered just what they would make of it. He had been told before not to bring the police to their house for any reason and he knew that this would cause a lot more trouble at home, just what he needed.   There was another interminable wait during which Martin had his fingerprints taken to help in elimination he was told which worried him about handling the knife.

The desk sergeant had hurried off and quickly organised some more men and then sent two out to the location Martin had described to them.

Within a short time they reported back that a murder had indeed been committed. They called in for assistance and told the sergeant that they had already called for a medical examiner to attend. Sergeant Wilson hurried off and found DCI Johnson and told him the news.

'All right, keep the lad here till I get back.' DCI Johnson said before hurrying out of the station, 'And call DS Smith for me, tell him to meet me there.'

1:45am Tuesday September 21st 1960

Murders were not all that common and DCI Johnson was keen to get on and investigate it. He was an experienced officer and at fifty years old was not long from retiring from the force. He was fit and broad, quite tall at six feet one. His greying brown hair was a little long reminding him that he must get it cut. He had what people would call a well lived in face, which was long and thin with a pointed nose and sharp bright grey eyes, he had a small moustache above his thin lips and there were lines around his eyes. He had started work for the force in London where he was born and over the years had been involved in many crimes including a few murders, some of which he had solved and some he hadn't. He had met a woman constable, Helen and eventually had married her. For some

36

time everything went really well and they tried for a family, which never happened. Tests then showed it was down to him that it hadn't. Helen could not get used to the fact of not having children and after a time the marriage failed and she left him for another man. Leonard never really got over it and he hadn't married again. There had been a few women he had been interested in but never let any of them get serious with him. He lived in an upmarket part of town in the suburbs and had all he wanted and needed and had got used to his lifestyle. He had a few male friends as well though not from the force, he liked to get away from all that in his own time. It all suited him quite well and meant he didn't have anyone to worry about anyone if he was working late. His colleagues were not so happy about that as it meant he would keep them out or pull them away from home without a thought about the time.

When he arrived at the scene he found three other police cars there and an ambulance. There was an officer at the alleyway entrance who lifted the tape that barred the alleyway as he entered and he made his way to the scene. There he found the medical examiner, Dr. Alan Price.

'What have we got Alan?' He asked.

Dr. Price got up from where he was kneeling beside the girl and answered, 'Young girl around fifteen, killed by multiple knife wounds, one piercing the heart, I would say a wide blade maybe five to six inches long, could be some kind of hunting knife. By the angle of the cuts I would say it was a right handed person. No signs of any sexual assault.' Alan Price rose slowly to his feet the arthritis in his knees causing him some difficulty. He was a small man with virtually no neck. He had a rounded face with very little hair left and was struggling now to control the size of his stomach. 'There was a struggle although it appears to have been very quick; all the cuts are from the front. There doesn't appear to be anything under the girl's fingernails or indeed anything else to help that I can see at the moment. No sign of the weapon used, or anything else as yet. I will know more later of course.'

'Alright, thanks Alan.' DCI Johnson knelt down to look at the girl; she was obviously young and was wearing quite nice clothes he thought. He wondered where she had been and where she had been heading. Coming down an alleyway like this didn't seem to fit in with her somehow.

'Alan, is there any sign that the body has been moved?'

'No, I am quite sure the murder occurred here.'

'What do you think the time of death would be?

Alan paused a moment before answering, ' Very recent, within the last three to four hours.' Alan replied as he packed his things away into his bag.

DCI Johnson thanked him then moved on to where two constables were standing moving out of the way of the photographer who was snapping away, "I want a door to door first thing in the morning, for now arrange a full search around these alleys and gardens, look for the murder weapon, footprints, anything that might help."

The two constables moved off to start work. At that moment another plain clothes man walked up.

'You took your time didn't you?' DCI Johnson said to him.

'Sorry sir, I was in bed, it was a long day yesterday.' DS Smith answered.

'Well it's going to be a long day today as well.' DCI Johnson added ruefully.

DS Smith grinned, yes he thought, it would certainly appear so. Detective Sergeant David Smith had been working for DCI Johnson for just a few months. He had found his boss to be hard working and strict but he was also fair with him and happy to offer help and assistance whenever he could which David was very appreciative of especially as he had high hopes of climbing up the ladder eventually.

David was younger by twenty years and around the same height and build as his boss. He had a shock of sandy hair that he could never quite keep in place, a young looking round face with laughter lines around his blue eyes. With a clean complexion he was often mistaken as being younger than he really was. He now felt nauseous as he always did when a murder case was presented to him. He hadn't been involved in that many but then one was enough. There had been one or two though and some of them had been really sickening. He had hoped when he got the call that this would be a false alarm or at least a quick clean death for the victim. If it was real then it would be another night he didn't get to go home. Judith would understand but then they had not been married long and it was always nice to get back home before their daughter Louise went to bed. She was only two and always wanted him to read her a bedtime story. Judith was understanding and had been right from the start but it was still hard to miss special occasions and have to be pulled out at night sometimes. David had grown up locally and had met Judith one evening while out with friends. It had been an immediate mutual attraction and in no time at all they were an item and were married within a year. They were happy and were busy building the home up. Having a daughter had just been the icing on the cake, she had been named Louise and they both loved her dearly. David spent as much time at home as he could but his job often had him out at all hours. However it was a job he loved and he wouldn't change it. He worked hard and tried to please his boss as well as being helpful and useful in solving the crimes they were faced with. He had always been the same and he supposed that was why he had achieved the position he was now at.

Looking at his boss now David asked, 'Who reported it?'

Leonard paused before answering, 'A young man came to the station, says he saw the whole thing.'

David's eyes lit up, 'Wow.' Is all he said.

Leonard turned to him, 'Aye and that's not all, he claims he followed the man to his house and has given us the address.'

'That is very convenient.'

'Isn't it. We will have to follow it up of course, as soon as we have finished here. Try to get an accurate time of death from Alan and what information you can from him and see how the search is going on and get anything they find bagged up in marked envelopes. Make sure they look very carefully. I want to see the photographs later too as soon as they are ready. I'm going to have a look around.'

DS David Smith could see the girl lying on the ground and asked, 'Do we have a name yet?'

'No, we don't have much at all at the moment. Check her pockets as soon as forensics have finished, maybe there will be something to help us.'

Leonard stepped back and looked at the scene, imagining it as Martin had described. He checked the gate where he had hidden in the garden and he could see how it could have happened exactly the way Martin had explained it. There were scuff marks on the ground where the lad could have been and what he had said seemed to tie up correctly. There were problems with his story however, like why he hadn't retrieved the knife? The girl was covered in blood so why was there none on him or his clothes? Things to sort out later he thought, for now he had to ensure all things possible were done here if they were going to be able to sort this out and find the perpetrator. The photographer was still taking photographs of everything and his men were searching carefully all around the scene.

Leonard was still looking around the alleyways when David came back up to him, 'No sign of the murder weapon, in fact very few signs of anything and interestingly no handbag or purse or anything on the girl.'

'Whoever murdered her could have taken a purse or whatever I suppose. Keep on with it, we may find something when it gets light and who knows maybe someone will have heard or seen something when we get the door to door going.'

'Ok, will do, this witness you have got sounds interesting though, he sounds like a clever lad, and to be on the scene ...'

'We will have a full statement from him when we get back and then we will follow up on this man he has told us about you can be sure of that. For now finish off what you can here then get back to the station. This young lad will need checking out carefully.'

As they spoke the girl was trolleyed out past them into the waiting ambulance. 'I'll send you the information as soon as I have it,' Alan told them as he passed. The two detectives nodded then got back to work.

Back at the station DCI Johnson read through Martin's statement then went back to see him. As he entered the room he said, 'We need to be more certain of what you saw.'

Martin was confused, 'You have found her then?' He asked sitting still and looking straight at the detective.

'Yes, we have.' Leonard Johnson said quietly.

'But the man, have you got him?'

Martin waited for him to carry on and when he didn't he asked, 'But you have been to the man's house as well haven't you?'

Leonard smiled, and walked up to Martin, 'We have no proof that it is him, there was nothing incriminating at the scene that we have found yet. We could arrange an identity parade but then you didn't see his face did you?'

'No, I didn't but I did follow him quite a way I am sure I could identify him again.'

'I don't think that would be enough from what you saw from behind. No we will have to carry out a lot of investigation yet but we will follow up on him don't you worry.'

Martin couldn't believe it, the man was going to get away with it and yet he had seen him murdering the girl, what was going on? 'What about the girl,' He asked, 'Have you taken her somewhere?'

'Never you mind about that, we have that all under control and her parents will be notified. Just don't go anywhere far away without telling us, we will be seeing you again. 'You can go home now but we will want to speak to you again very soon.'

Martin walked out of the station unsure of what to do next. He supposed he ought to go back home. No doubt the police will be round tomorrow or the next day as they said and then it will all start again at home with his parents, the shouting, the anger. They would certainly not like the police knocking on their door. Martin sighed as he trudged home. He was tired and hungry. The officer had given him a cheese sandwich with his second cup of tea as well as some biscuits but his tummy was telling him that it wasn't enough.

Eventually he got home, raided the kitchen again then went to bed and fell asleep straight away as soon as his head hit the pillow.

He woke suddenly and remembered the events of the night and grabbed his bedside clock. The fingers were showing 7.30am. Groggily he rose, still in his clothes. Something was wrong, very wrong, why hadn't the police arrested the man, the murderer? Then he realised, there was only one thing to do, as they had no proof they couldn't do anything. He had to get some proof himself; they would believe him then and arrest the man, yes that is what he would have to do. The murderer had taken the girls bag with him and the knife and possibly he still had them hidden away somewhere, somewhere in his house most likely. Even if the police went to the house and had a look around it wouldn't have been hard for the man to have hide things somewhere where they wouldn't look, not without a full search anyway and as yet he didn't think they would do that not without a warrant anyway. So it was all down to him. Martin knew he had to go back to where the man lived and somehow get in and find some proof and take it to the police. Maybe he could get the man's fingerprints on something, especially if he could find the knife. It would have the man's on as well as his own, as he hadn't worn gloves when he had killed the girl. Then they would know it was him and go and arrest him. In the back of his mind Martin wondered why he had killed her. She was so much smaller than him, why did he have to do that? He could obviously have overpowered her easily. And what was she doing in the alleyway at night in the first place? It all seemed very odd to him, surely the man could have found a victim that would be more rewarding than her, well the answer to that would have to wait, for now he had to get back to the house and wait until the man went out then he would get in somehow and take a look around.

Martin had a quick wash then he went to the kitchen to get some breakfast which he needed as he suspected it was going to be a long day. There he found his mother making some toast.

'Is dad up yet? Martin asked cautiously as he walked in.

'Huh, what do you think, it's a bit early yet for him?' That was exactly what Martin thought but it paid to be sure of these things. He put the kettle on and prepared two cups while his mum carried on making the toast. She was busy with her own thoughts standing there in her dressing gown and slippers her short brown hair a mess, not yet combed. She looked older than she was at forty one years old. Once she had looked quite pretty, slim with long hair, a rounded face with full lips and had the lads all after her, now though after living with her husband Jim for the last twenty years she had let herself go, after all he never noticed or bothered what she looked like and they never went anywhere together much so why should she bother?

'Are you out again today?' She asked while buttering the toast.

'Er, yes, possibly all day.' He found it interesting that she hadn't asked about where he was last night or that she hadn't noticed or at least mentioned how late it was when he had returned home.

'There must be some jobs about for you surely? You need to find one soon, for one thing I need your board money. I presume that is what you are going to do today is it, look for a job?' She looked straight at him while she put the toast on a plate on the table and poured out a cup of tea.

Martin was happy for her to think that he would be out job hunting. 'It's not that easy to find a job mum. I have some ideas to try today though. I know I need to get some work somewhere but it's hard to find anything suitable.'

'Anything suitable. I would have thought that anything would do, at least for now, you can always look around again once you have got something. You just can't go on slumming around. I need to get something off you each week. It's not a hotel you know.'

43

Martin didn't answer that. He just ate his toast as quickly as he could then without his mum noticing he went down to the cellar where his dad kept his tools. There he rummaged around and found a screwdriver and a pair of pliers which he pocketed as well as a couple of other things he wanted. Back in his room he gathered a torch and a few other things he needed which he crammed into his pockets then quietly he left the house and set off purposefully.

8.00am Tuesday September 21st 1960

Leonard and David sat together at Leonard's desk to go over what they had.

Leonard looked up from the report folder, 'The most interesting thing we have is this statement from Martin Baxter. He is certain of what he saw so what we will do now is pay this man a call and see what he has to say for himself.'

'That sounds good to me sir.' David replied.

'But that is for later, first we have another call to make.' Both men looked sombre at this. 'It appears the murder victim is Julie West, fifteen years old, she lived locally and apparently was reported missing some hours ago by her Mother who we now need to visit first.' Leonard put the folder back in his in tray and together they left the office.

The dead girl's parents lived a little way off but it was only minutes later that DCI Johnson and DS Smith arrived at their house. Leonard Johnson made the introductions and he felt his stomach turn as they were invited into the living room.

'You have news of Julie officer, is she all right?' Mrs West asked straight away as she ushered them in.

It was always awful to be the one to give bad news such as this and no amount of experience seemed to help. Leonard was happy that it didn't happen that often but to tell someone that one of their kin was dead was a task no one ever wanted to do. It always reminded him of how cruel the world and people could be.

The West's house was a terraced building like all the others in the street and in the area and it was immaculate inside. Mrs West was obviously proud of her home and kept it very clean and tidy. The room they were in had a sofa in the middle facing a large tiled fireplace with a coal fire brightly burning away. There were two armchairs placed to either side and a television on a table in a corner. Chintzy curtains hung at the windows tied back neatly. A sideboard held a clock and various ornaments, altogether giving the room a real homely warm feeling. Leonard could imagine the girl being here and being happy with her life and now it was over.

Leonard stood in front of Mrs West as her husband entered the room, David stood to one side. Leonard always thought there was only one way to handle these situations and was to come straight out with it.

'I am sorry to tell you Mrs West that a girl has been found in an alleyway close to here who bears the description of your daughter.'

'How do you mean found inspector?' Mr West asked.

Leonard turned to him and answered, 'I'm sorry sir but it's the body of a dead girl.'

Mrs West's face changed from questioning to horror before she said, 'Are you sure it is her?'

'Could you tell us what she was wearing tonight?'

Slightly flummoxed Mrs West answered, 'She had a flowered dress on, blue. A scarf and I think a little leather jacket.'

Leonard nodded. I am really sorry but that makes us as sure as we can be at this time that it is Julie, we will need you to come and make a formal identification but it would appear to be her yes.'

Mrs West broke up and cried on her husband's shoulder. 'Why, why her, my beautiful little girl? 'She sobbed.

'We can't answer that Mrs West I'm sorry, but we will do everything we can to bring her killer to justice.' Leonard said.

'How did it happen?' Mr West asked. Putting an arm around his wife and holding her close. She was a lot shorter than him with her blond hair permed neatly and Leonard thought how surreal this was seeing her standing there in her flowered dress with her husband who was dressed very smartly although casual in brown twill trousers and slippers with a striped jumper. They obviously lived quite well even though they were in this area of town.

Leonard hesitated before saying, 'I'm sorry Mr West but she was stabbed, once through the heart, it would have been quick. Can we sit down, Mr West maybe a cup of tea for your wife.'

'Yes, of course,' Mr West beckoned the sofa then slowly walked out of the room. Mrs West sank into an armchair.

'Stabbed! But who, who would do such a thing.' Mrs West was beside herself and could hardly talk through her tears.

There was little that Leonard could say to her but he carried on with, 'It makes no sense I agree, these things unfortunately do happen of course and we will do all we can to find out who and why.'

When Mr West returned and had given Mrs West her cup and the officers theirs, Leonard said, 'I am really sorry to ask but we need to know all we can as soon as we can to help us find whoever did this. Can you tell us where she was this evening?'

'She was with friends detective, a birthday party of a close friend of hers, Sheila Hobbs.' Mr West answered for them both as he wiped his black hair from his forehead.

'Where was this?' David asked, his notebook in his hand.

'Just a few streets away, off Osmaston Road.' Mr West paused and put his head in his hands for a few moments.

David took the address from him then asked, 'Did she go with anyone?'

Mrs West, looked up and answered, 'No, she went alone, she has been there before, quite often in fact, they were best friends, we thought she would be safe, she always was before. When it got late we rang them up and they said she had left some time earlier, we went out and looked around but couldn't see her so that's when I rang the police and reported her missing.'

Leonard took over the questioning, 'Do you have a recent photo, it could be useful?' Mrs West opened a cupboard and removed one from an album, 'You will return it won't you?' She asked earnestly.

'Of course.' Leonard answered, 'I will have it copied and returned to you.'

'Do you have any clues yet?' Mr West asked.

Leonard looked at David before answering, 'There are a couple of leads we need to follow up on but it is too early yet to say what use they will be. Why would Julie come home down the alleyway?'

Mr West looked up, tears in his eyes, 'She always did, we all use them, it's a shortcut, saves walking all the way round to the main road. It's always been safe.' He sobbed a little, 'Until now.'

David asked, 'Did she have a handbag or a purse with her?'

Mrs West looked at him disbelievingly, 'Of course she was killed for her money, but she didn't have any, well not much anyway.' She thought for a moment before continuing, 'Yes she had a handbag, it was only a little one, purple I think with white flowers on. She would have her purse with her, but there wouldn't be much in it, I don't think she normally carries any money with her to her friend's house anyway.' She said breaking down again.

'Surely she wouldn't have been killed for that.' Mr West said. Then he paused and looked closely at Leonard, 'Unless, was she...? ' He began.

Leonard interrupted with, 'There is no sign of a sexual attack it all seems to have been very hurried. She didn't have much time to struggle and we don't know yet as to the motive.'

'We didn't find a handbag or a purse so it seems logical that the killer would have taken them.'

'We will need one of you to make a formal identification.' David reminded them.

Mr West sighed and said, 'Of course I will do it.'

'Thank you Mr West. Sometime today would be good if you would.'

'Of course, just tell me when and where.'

'These friends of hers Mr West, where they male or female?' Leonard asked.

'I'm not sure. It was a girl friend's birthday, Sheila Hobbs, but I don't know who else was there, possibly both. Sheila was her best friend they did everything together, she would know.'

'You say they were always together?'

'Virtually inseparable, Sheila was always around here or Julie round at hers, they got on really well together.'

'What about boyfriends?' Leonard carried on.

'She has had one or two, not at the moment to our knowledge, mostly from school, but nothing serious I'm sure.' Mrs West said, mopping tears from her face. She looked at Leonard, her eyes swollen and red.

'We will need to know names and anything else you can tell us.' Leonard carried on.

'You think a boyfriend did this? Mr West asked shocked.

'At the moment we can't rule anything out.' Looking at the couple Leonard knew they needed time to take it all in but he also needed information, 'If you can, now would be a good time to tell us all you know.' He said this gently and watched the reaction.

They both straightened up and Mr West said, 'We will tell you what we can, whoever did this needs catching.'

Leonard thanked him and allowed David to take over asking questions and making notes as the answers came while he thought of how he was going to keep the press at bay while he sorted it all out.

Then Leonard asked, 'We will need to see Julie's room.'

'Whatever for Inspector?' Mrs West asked.

'She may have known her attacker, there may be evidence there that we can use to help us track her killer.'

Mrs West just shrugged and led the way upstairs. She opened the door to Julie's room then stood there as the two men entered.

Leonard looked at her and said, 'Thank you Mrs West, we can manage now.'

Taking the hint she went out and closed the door.

'Right David, look carefully before touching anything but search everywhere.'

'Yes sir,' David answered opening dressing table drawers.

The room was a reasonable size and was very tidy for a teenage girl. The wallpaper was fresh and modern; light blue with white stripes the carpet multicoloured. There was a single bed with a metal frame, with a bedside cabinet beside it, a teak wardrobe and matching chest of drawers along one wall. There was also a comfy armchair, a small table with a record player on it and a straight backed chair. Around the walls were several pictures, all amateurish and on examination they all had Julie's signature on them.

Together they searched around until Leonard eventually found a diary tucked under some scarves and gloves at the bottom of her bedside cabinet. He started opening the pages and reading through it. After a few moments he stopped and called David over.

'David, come and look at this.' He said.

David leaned over then caught what Leonard was referring to, 'There are pages missing.' He said incredulously.

'Exactly, and most of them recently, look around see if you can find any of them.'

Together they searched and although they were meticulous they did not find any of them or anything else except when Leonard opened her wardrobe and looking around he remarked, 'For a young girl of fifteen she seems to have had a rather expensive taste in clothes.'

They both looked and saw designer dresses and shoes, and interestingly they were all hidden at the end of the rail or buried under other items. She had put coats and obviously older clothes over the top of designer items on hangers. Expensive shoes were in boxes under older shoes at the bottom of the wardrobe.

'It looks like her mother doesn't know about these.' David said.

'No I'm sure she doesn't,' Leonard mused, 'I wonder why not and where the money came from to buy them? Come on and bring that diary with you David.'

When they returned downstairs Leonard asked Mr West, 'How much weekly pocket money did Julie get?'

'Why on earth do you want to know that?'

Leonard was ready for that answer, 'It would help us to work out what circles of people she was mixing with and where she was able to go.'

'Hmm, well it varied a bit, she would get more at certain times depending on what was happening but usually a pound a week.'

Leonard thought that was quite reasonable but not enough to obtain what he had just seen upstairs.

'Mrs West we want to take Julie's diary with us to check through, we will bring it back to you as soon as we can.'

'Her diary, why is there something important in it?'

'It's hard to say at the moment but it may be useful.'

'I will want it back.' Mrs West was getting more upset.

'Of course, we won't keep it any longer that we have to.'

Mrs West had to be happy with that and Leonard promised to keep them informed of any developments and having arranged for Mr West to perform a formal identification they both left.

When they got outside Leonard spoke about it with David, 'There is something rather odd there, where was she getting the money from for those clothes?'

David didn't know although he made suggestions that Leonard didn't agree with.

'Something else to consider and we need to look into those missing diary pages, maybe there will be something in the rest of the diary to help us with that.' Leonard said as they drove off. 'Now for a very different sort of visit.'

* * *

As Leonard pulled up at the curb two houses before number twenty three two miles away from the station they both took in the state of the building, 'Not the most well looked after is it?' He said.

'No sir, I wonder what we will find inside?' David remarked.

'We will soon find out,' Leonard said getting out of the car.

Nathaniel Armstrong was sitting in a chair by an upstairs window overlooking the street as he often did in the mornings. It was a quiet time for him for if he was working then he would be out normally all night or maybe get a few hours sleep and this would his time to relax and think things through before having something to eat and then getting his head down again for a few hours. This morning however there was to be no rest. He banged down his empty whisky glass on the small table beside him and stood up. The knock on door had come as a surprise, a shock even. He had seen the car pull up and two men get out but he no idea that they were going to knock on his door or who they were.

Could it be that he had been rumbled, he doubted it could be possible but then why were they here, were they indeed police? It seemed most likely. The knock came again more insistent this time. He gave a quick look around then slowly he made his way downstairs. It was early for him to be up usually at this time, the truth was he hadn't been to bed at all that night. He checked his appearance in the hall mirror and satisfied with what he saw then he went and opened the door.

Both men showed their warrant cards and gave their names.

'What can I do for you?' Nathanial asked politely.

'Could we come in sir, we would like a little chat if that's all right?'

'What's it all about?'

'Just routine, if you wouldn't mind sir, it won't take long.' Leonard said standing very close to the door with David close behind him.

Nathanial shrugged and stepped aside allowing them to enter the hall. 'You can come in here,' Nathanial said leading the way into a small living room at the front of the house.

Leonard strode in and stood in front of the window followed by Nathanial while David stood by the door. Nathanial sat in an armchair, crossed his legs and beckoned the sofa to them. Leonard sat while David remained standing. Both men noticed that the room was obviously hardly used, there was dust on the few items of furniture and there was a slight smell of damp. There was a sofa, an armchair in the middle of the room and a long sideboard along the door wall with a few old ornaments on it, nothing of any value or looked to have been used recently.

'Can you tell us where you were from eight until ten o'clock last night?' Leonard asked.

Nathanial looked closely at him and slowly answered, 'I was here watching television, why do you want to know?'

Leonard ignored the question and carried on, 'We have someone who says you were somewhere else mister er...?'

Nathanial feigned surprise, 'I was somewhere else, who says so, they are a liar, I was here as I say?'

'Could we have your name please sir,' David interjected.

'It's Nathanial Armstrong, now do you mind telling me what it is I am supposed to have done or where I was supposed to be?' He voice raising and stern.

Leonard sat on the edge of the sofa and tried to gauge the man he was looking at, his face told him nothing, there was no surprise, no fear, this man was very sure of himself which in itself told him something, 'We are investigating a murder which took place last night at around that time.'

'What and you think I did it?' Nathanial's face turned into a sneer. Who says so?'

'That I can't say but someone answering your description was seen at the scene and we have to follow up all the information we get.'

'Well it wasn't me, I have been in all night.'

'Do you have anyone who could confirm that sir,' David asked.

Nathanial took his time to turn and look at him, 'No I don't. I don't usually invite people into my home sergeant.'

'Do you own a black overcoat and a trilby hat sir?' Leonard carried on.

Nathanial's face froze before splitting into a grin, so here it was, now for the test of just how clever he was, 'I can't say I have, I have a dark blue overcoat that's true, but a trilby no, now what would I look like wearing one of those?'

'Do you mind if we take a look around sir,' David asked.

'I do mind, why should I let you two come in here accusing me of murder of all things and now you want to search my home on the word of someone who's name you won't say?' Nathanial's voice again rose as he spoke.

'We are not accusing you of anything sir we just have to do our duty and check out all ends and leads we have.' Leonard said quietly.

Nathanial sat for a moment then said, 'All right, yes, go on you can have a look, not that you will find anything, but if it puts your mind at rest go ahead.' Nathanial rose and went towards the door.

David got there before him and opened it, 'Maybe you could show us round sir,' He said.

Nathanial eased back then led the way from the room. He showed them into every room in the house and let them take a look around. They even went through his wardrobe. Nathanial stood back each time smiling inwardly to himself. After a while they ended up back at the front door.

'Thank you Mister Armstrong that was very obliging of you.' Leonard said.

'Yeah well, there you go now maybe you will leave me in peace, whatever someone has said to you they were wrong, go looking for your man elsewhere.' Nathanial closed the door firmly behind them.

'Not the most likeable kind of person was he sir,' David said as they walked back to the car.

'No, he wasn't. That doesn't make him a murderer though although there was something about him, no real surprise at our questions, a strange sort of a man. He was so calm when I mentioned the murder, not

54

a normal reaction and he didn't ask about the murder victim either which was rather odd.'

'That's what I thought, something not quite right but nothing you can put your finger on sir.' David said as he opened the car door.

'No, there was definitely something weird about him but as I say that doesn't make him a murderer. Come on let's get back to the station I want to have another look at that boys statement.' Leonard said thoughtfully.

'You don't suppose that the boy did do it and is trying to pass on the blame do you sir?'

'Always a possibility, I suppose he could have something against this person and is blaming him. That is something we will have to check out. It looks like we have work to do, and something tells me this is going to be a difficult case even though we have the name and address of the murderer, which to say the least is unusual if indeed it is him.'

* * *

Nathaniel was very angry, angry and upset that he had allowed this to happen. It was going to take him a while to get over the surprise of when the police had knocked on his door. At first he thought that the game was up but then it soon became apparent that they had nothing on him, only the rantings of a boy who had no proof against him. That boy, God if only he had have caught him! He was going to have to look out for him, go back to that area at some time soon and see if he could see him again. It would be hard to recognise him although he was sure he would know him by his clothes but even then there was no guarantee that he would wear them again. Even so he was pretty sure he would know him if he saw him, he must be a local surely. He certainly knew his way around. He had been very clever to avoid him and even more so to follow him home after all the precautions he had taken to ensure that he was not followed. He picked up the whisky bottle from the table, filled his glass and took another long swallow.

Nathaniel Armstrong was forty two years old and he was a lonely secretive man. He was quite tall at five feet eleven and very bulky and strong. He kept himself as fit as he could although he didn't worry too much about his appearance, after all who was there to look good for? He had no wife and hadn't had a girlfriend in many long years. Unsociable and quiet and he had found it virtually impossible to get anyone to like him and he had now given up with finding anyone to share his life with. He was moody and had anger swings especially when the unexpected happened like just now. Standing by the window he looked at himself in the reflection and saw his face that was long and lean that needed a shave with thick brown eyebrows and high cheek bones, the nose was also long and thin, the mouth small, showing hardly any lips and his skin was white from seeing hardly any sunlight. His black hair was starting to thin and grey patches were starting appear, he had it swept over his head which helped to hide his face but it was the eyes that took his attention, they were big and round and dark giving a menacing look that showing no emotion and seemed to burn back at him.

His mother had died of cancer when he was just ten years old and he had been brought up by his father who was a mechanical engineer by trade and was very meticulous about everything which drove Nathanial mad. Everything had to be in its place, everywhere kept spotlessly clean including Nathanial and of course their clothes. Nathanial had thought that this was his father's way of coping without his mother but as time went on he never changed. Then when Nathanial was just sixteen his father had a massive heart attack and had died in the house one evening. The shock and the follow up of everything that had to be done was a big load for Nathanial. Neither of his parents had any siblings as indeed he didn't either so there were very few people to rally round and help him. In the end he managed somehow to do it all himself while at the same time trying to hold down a job he had at a local bicycle shop. That was another thing that hadn't gone down too well with his father as he had wanted him to take up engineering as he had but Nathanial was just not interested and took the bicycle shop job just to fill in until something better came along, which of course it never did.

He has lost that job within a few months of his father's death and had tried a few others before giving up and turning to crime. Why should he work his socks off when crime was so much easier he had argued with himself? He had become angrier and more uncontrollable as the years had passed and now he thought that the world owed him, owed him whatever he could get. Not being able to hold any job down and turning to crime he had tried minor thefts at first and then more and more daring deeds followed. As time went on and he remained at large he began to wonder how long his luck would last and then one night he decided to mug a man he watched leaving a bank. He hoped that the man had made a withdrawal not a deposit, which proved to be the case. He jumped the man from behind and a fight ensued as the man unexpectedly fought back and then unfortunately the man got a good look at his face. Suddenly Nathaniel realised that this time he could be recognised and it would all come out about his previous deeds. In a rush of excitement and desperation he knifed the man again and again his adrenalin keeping him on. The knife had been something he had carried for a long while, as defence at first but then to threaten with. Being introverted and nervous he had bought a hunting knife a few years ago. The blade was just six inches long but it was thick strong fluted metal with a wicked edge and a bone handle. After stealing the man's money he had ran off pocketing the knife.

The killing was something he wished he not done but he had little remorse, the man shouldn't have fought back and there was no going back now so over the years he had committed more burglaries, more muggings and thefts from cars often using the knife to threaten his victims with. Now he was always careful to cover his face with something, usually a scarf so he couldn't be identified. He didn't keep to the same area but often caught a bus to another town to do his dirty work. He didn't own a car or indeed wanted one, that would mean paperwork that could be traced back to him if the car was seen while he was doing a job so he kept to buses and trains or just walked.

In between he would sometimes get a little job to take a rest from his crimes sometimes for long periods, which helped to keep the police off his tracks. They were always mundane jobs where he wouldn't have to make friends or mix with the public, manual labouring, the bike repair shop, those kind of things.

Living alone had the advantage of him being able to come and go as he wished with no one to bother about or explain to but it also had the disadvantage of having no one to turn to, no one to help him or even to talk to. He had sunk into a self depreciating cycle making him bitter and resentful of virtually everyone with no thought for anyone but himself.

He was really sorry about the girl tonight though; she had been such an easy soft target right from the start. He had never expected to find her or anyone like her. She asked him to let her go and they had argued for a minute before Nathanial had lost his temper. She was of course no match for him and he soon had her on the ground. He had no plan of what to do with her but then he tried to remove her scarf to gag her with to stop her making so much noise. There was also a chance of using her stockings too to restrain her with but then in the struggle she managed to reach up and pull his scarf down revealing his face to her which she reached up to scratch. Nathanial's anger had surged again and the knife had been in his hand before he had realised it. Again and again he plunged it into her until she fell limp away from him. It was then he had noticed the boy. That blasted boy, why the hell had he been there at that time of night anyway, unless of course he was on the same mission as he was to find somewhere to burgle?

He realised now that the boy must have managed somehow to follow him home although that was quite amazing as he was always so careful about coming and going from a crime and would go in circles often stopping and waiting on the way to make sure that he was not being followed, but this time he had been. Now the boy knew where he lived. That would require some thought. Carefully he eased back to the window and from one side looked out into the street. Would he have the nerve to be out there now or come looking for him again, and what if he did? This is something he knew he must resolve, but that would have to wait until later, now he had to rest and see what tomorrow would bring. For now he crossed the room and opened a cupboard built into the wall. Walking to the left far corner he knelt down pulled away a pile of cardboard boxes that filled the corner and pulled away at a crack in the woodwork on the wall enabling some boards to be removed to reveal a space that was under the stairs that went up to a small attic. Looking into the space he checked that the knife was there together with his stash of money collected so painfully over the years. Some of it he had spent but there was still a substantial amount left that he may need as time went on, especially for when he was too old to work. His coat, scarf and hat were also in there as well as the handbag he had taken from the girl which was something he would have to dispose of tomorrow. He had taken it in case there was anything in it of importance, any money in it was immaterial but there was nothing of any interest only some makeup and a few coins in a small purse. There was also the house key he had retrieved from a jacket pocket. Tired now he put the boards back and retired to bed.

8.30am Tuesday September 21st 1960

Martin stopped at the end of Winston Street, unsure now where to position himself. He needed to wait and see if the man left the house although he couldn't be sure that he hadn't already left. Carefully he looked up and down the street especially to the right where he knew the man's house was. The houses were all drab red brick palisaded, very similar to his own, which he knew the man's to be, and there were also some terraced much like those on his street. There was also a shop on the opposite side near the main road which gave Martin mixed feelings, Useful as it was for somewhere to go and hide out it would mean more people may be about that may wonder why he was hanging around. There was always the open ground at the end of the street and that looked most promising although it would not give him a very good view of the front of the house. If he waited there he would just have to watch for the man in the street rather than exiting the house.

Carefully he started down the street, not hurrying, not dawdling and keeping his eyes and senses on alert for any sign of the man or for anyone who may see him walking, the less that did the better he thought. Only two other people passed him down the street and Martin guessed they were on their way to work and they paid him no attention. He had walked right up to the house before he realised it and slowed down to get a good look at the front of the building. It had a fancy designed Victorian palisaded frontage with a short garden that was unkempt. There was a wooden fence at the pavement with no gate to the path up to the front door, which looked very strong and imposing. The curtains were drawn on the downstairs and upstairs windows and there were no lights on giving him no clues as to what was inside and there was no way of telling whether the man was in there or not. The garden area had bushes in front of the house and it was quite weeded up. Martin took all this in quickly and wondered what his chances were of hiding amongst the bushes. Maybe that would be possible at night but now, he wasn't sure that they would give him enough cover and he walked on. As he passed by he noticed the entrance to the alleyway and stopped. In between the houses there were alleyways allowing access to the back gardens. That was just what he needed. Looking round and making sure that no one was watching he made his way down the alley.

It began as a tunnel under the upstairs rooms until it reached the back of the houses where the back gardens began. Here there were six foot high brick walls to either side and Martin stopped there and tried to look over into the neighbour's garden to see if anyone was there who might see him but it looked quiet enough so he walked on. Once he was a few feet further on he stopped and looked around and over the wall to the upstairs bedrooms of the man's house. Here the curtains were drawn as well and there was no sign of life. Martin didn't know whether that was a good thing or not. At least it meant he wouldn't be seen while he investigated further. The alley went on between the brick walls to the end of the gardens. Here it came to a junction where another alley went behind the back walls of the houses to either side. Behind them was a higher wall and behind that trees and bushes that were quite high and behind them the gardens of the houses that backed up to these gardens from the next street.

Martin was pleased to get around the corner and behind the man's garden out of sight from the alley and the house next door. A few feet further on was the gate to the garden. Here he stopped and thought of what to do next. Carefully he tried the handle, which moved, but the gate did not open. Looking over the gate he could see the back upstairs windows of the house and indeed those of several houses to either side, seeing nothing untoward he pulled himself up the gate and felt over the top for any sign of a bolt or other lock. To his surprise there was a bolt, which wouldn't open. The door had obviously dropped and the bolt was stuck. Thankful that he had brought some tools with him Martin got to work with the pliers and screwdriver and after a few minutes struggle the bolt opened after a hard tug. Pushing on the gate he found it to be stiff on rusty hinges and it dragged on the ground making a protesting screeching noise but after a few inches it opened easily enough and allowed Martin to see into the garden. He peered in around the gate and could now see a jungle of plants, bushes and young trees; this man was obviously not a gardener. However, it worked to Martin's advantage and he crept in keeping his profile as small as possible and bending over he moved up towards the house. He was able to hide very easily among the bushes and trees and he quickly got to within a couple of yards from the kitchen window. Here the curtains were open and he risked going up for a look through the window. The door from the kitchen to the rest of the house was closed so he felt fairly safe in doing so. It was a fair sized room with all the usual fittings although nothing looked particularly clean. The thing that interested Martin the most was whether he could force an entrance through the door or window when and if an opportunity arrived.

It was obvious straight away that either would make a lot of noise. The door was well locked and of solid wood that would take a while to open. The kitchen windows were all shut tight and they would have to be broken. He stepped back and looked again. The kitchen was only half the width of the building and there was a paved area at the side, which led up to another door, which was at the side of the building and the windows of the downstairs and upstairs rooms which all had the curtains drawn. He crept up to this point and paused and listened carefully for any sounds for a few minutes his heart beating wildly before he checked the door, it was locked and again it would be noisy to gain entrance through there but when he looked up he could see that the bedroom window above was slightly ajar, that he thought was very lucky but how to get at it? He had no intention of going in when he wasn't sure if it was safe but he needed to know a way when the situation arose. The only way appeared to be up a metal drainpipe that ran down the wall quite close to the window. He was sure that with a little effort he would be able to climb up and gain access there so then as quietly and as carefully as he could he went back down the garden to the back alley and closed the gate.

Very soon he was back out on the street feeling more confident now that he had taken the chance to have a good look around. All he had to do now was find somewhere where he wouldn't be seen and wait for the man to go out again. The problems were, where and for how long? Then it came to him, across the street a few houses up there was one for sale, which appeared to be empty. Thanking his lucky stars he went over and a cursory look through the windows proved that it was vacant. Keeping an eye out he went into the alleyway at the side far enough in to be out of sight from the street but keeping an angle to keep the house front of number twenty three in sight.

He thought now that he may have to wait for quite a while. He only had the bottle of water and the few biscuits he had brought from home with him but they would have to do. He sat down on the brick floor and rested his back against the wall and thought of what to say if the neighbour to the house of the alley he was in came and saw him. That he decided was something he would just have to come up with if the situation arose.

Time passed by and nothing happened, the curtains stayed closed and the house stayed quiet. He thought that maybe the man only came out at night in which case he had a long wait to endure with very little to eat or drink.

10.00am Tuesday September 21st 1960

Josephine sat despondently on a bench in the Arboretum. She had been there for some time now and was unsure of what to do next. She was hungry and there was nothing left in her rucksack to eat or drink. She got up and started walking. She enjoyed walking around the park, although it was cold the sun did make an occasional appearance making everywhere look so much better. She liked to hear the birds in the trees and see the flowers. They looked so nice and it all took her mind off her troubles. She stopped at the aviaries and watched the birds for a while before moving on. There were budgies very noisily flying around in one pen. The next had parakeets with many colours and on the ground where pheasants and other birds. The last one had parrots, which whistled and imitated what they had heard from the visitors. After a little while thirst made her leave there and continue walking around the park. She walked past two gardeners working at clearing a flowerbed ready for winter flowers to go in and looked longingly at their flasks, which she suspected contained hot tea. Eventually she reached the orangery hothouse further on and she was thankful to find a cold water tap that was in there for the gardeners. She filled the empty fruit juice bottle she had with her and took a long drink, at least that was something she thought. Food would have to wait.

Sitting on a bench in there was better, she was now out of the wind and it was a good place to be if it rained she thought. She sat there relaxing and stretched her legs out. She began thinking of the homes she had been in and the people who had cared for her. Only a few of the foster parents that she had known could she think of kindly. Mostly they just wanted the money for looking after her and hadn't really cared for her and she had always ended up back in a care home somewhere after a short while. Unruly they called her, rude and difficult to handle. Well, that is how they considered her, Josephine thought she was just doing what she could to survive plus she was angry, angry at being in the situation she was in, no home, no family, no friends, no future, no job, no money. Was it any wonder she was difficult to live with? At her age she was too old now to be fostered anyway and the home she was in was badgering her to get a job and they were looking for somewhere else for her to stay, that all sounded good enough but not with the creep who worked there and no doubt would have a good say in where she went to and he would be involved with that as well, too involved she thought.

Only one couple were really kind to her, they were older than any of the others she had been with and had a calm demeanour which helped Josephine to settle in with them. Mr and Mrs Freeman had decided to take her in and give her a good life. It had been difficult at first for her and for them as Josephine had to adjust to her new surroundings and routines but as she got used to it all she became really happy and contented. They lived in a big house with a large garden and Josephine did well there. They bought her clothes and all manner of things and she had a nice room all to herself. Everything was perfect. She started at a local school and did well in her studies, which pleased her and her foster parents. It was all too good to be true and Josephine thought she had finally landed on her feet and would be all right from then on. She made a few friends in the area who she could take back to the house. The foster parents were very caring but also gave her room in which to move and express herself, attributes that she hadn't had anywhere else or since. Everything would have been ok and she probably would have been able to make something of herself living with them only for what happened after almost a year of happiness. That was when Mrs Johnson suddenly became very ill and Mr Johnson found that he was no longer able to carry on caring for her as his wife was taking up all his time. Josephine was very sorry to leave. There were many tears but she had to go back into a care home and after that none of the people she was placed with ever came anywhere near the care she had experienced and she again went off the rails.

Thinking about the past wouldn't help; she came out of her reverie and looked around. She couldn't stay here all day; she had to move on but where to? She had only been partly prepared when she had had to leave the care home and hadn't thought ahead but now her thoughts turned to the railway station, maybe she could get away, far away from the home and the risk of being taken back there and who knows what then? First though how to board a train with no money? She checked her purse. There was only a one pound note and a few coppers, hardly enough to get her anywhere. Still she trudged on through the town towards the station hoping that something would crop up or that she would find a way to board a train without a ticket. Otherwise she didn't have a clue where to go or what to do next.

She walked down the main road passing many shops and spent her pound on some sandwiches and a chocolate bar, which she put in her rucksack for later. What good was a pound anyway for a train ride she thought? She wondered how on earth she was going to get any more money and the thought of stealing some did occur to her but how hard was that going to be plus it was something she did not want to do and never had done before but then if that was the only way then maybe. She really would have to wait and see how things turned out.

Eventually she arrived at the railway station and went up to the notice board for trains, and studied their destinations and prices. Well, she thought, I am definitely going to need some more money if I am going to get away by train. She looked at getting onto the platform and on to a train but there were turnstiles and people watching and officials checking for tickets. There was no way for her to get through so gloomily she turned away and headed out of the station.

She thought that the care workers may well have missed her by now as Mr Henderson would no doubt have put out an alarm once he had got into her room and found her and her things missing and no doubt they would have informed the police as well and they would be out looking for her. Maybe the train station was not a good place to hide while thinking it through so she quickly moved off along the streets, glancing over her shoulder occasionally as she went. Her steps took her to an Industrial Estate where there were many buildings not in use. A search around here soon found her a door ajar to a large abandoned workshop area. She pushed at it until it opened far enough for her to enter and she slipped inside. It was not clean or warm but it was out of the wind and the miserly rain that occasionally showered down. She shouldered the door shut and took a look around. There was litter over the concrete floor and a high ceiling with rusting lamps hanging down. There were other entrances too but she discovered that they were all locked up which was probably a good thing. Maybe someone else had been able to force the door she had come in by and then left by now as there was no sign of anyone having been there. She went back to the door and ensured it was properly closed in case anyone else came then looked around and found a length of steel, which she used to prop the door shut just in case whoever had forced an entry came back again, or anyone else for that matter. Looking around she found some large cardboard boxes strewn on the floor and gratefully she piled them up in a corner and made herself somewhere to rest up. She settled herself down and made herself as comfortable as she could then began to eat her sandwiches her mind on the shops she had passed earlier.

* * *

DCI Leonard Johnson and DS David Smith had spent some time checking through Martin's statement and gathering the information from the medical examiner and from the officers who had conducted a house to house enquiry. Now it was all laid out in front of them on Leonard's desk together with the photographs.

Together they sat at Leonard's desk amidst the pile of paperwork there for them to work through.

'Anything from the house to house David?' Leonard asked.

'Nothing sir, nobody saw or heard anything. Nothing else of any real interest from the medical examiner either. Nothing to help us solve the crime anyway. On the face of it this looks like it could be have been an opportunist mugging. With no witnesses, nothing to go on and nothing on the girl to help us.' David said.

'I not sure about a mugging; on a young girl?' No something isn't right, I mean why would a man like Nathanial or anyone really attack and kill a girl for what might have been in her handbag?' Leonard sat with his legs crossed as he twiddled a pencil in his fingers.

'Maybe a man like Nathanial wouldn't but the boy, well you never know. Maybe he wanted more than what was in the handbag?' David answered swallowing the last dregs of tea from his cup.

Leonard looked up and stared for a minute, 'That is possible of course yes and it does appear as though an attempt was made to gag or tie her with her own scarf.'

'Which means he hadn't come prepared, maybe it was just coincidental that they met up there, or maybe he knew she would be going down that alleyway but then why would he be carrying a knife, especially a hunting knife, a penknife or a kitchen knife is one thing but a hunting knife, that implies premeditation?'

'Yes it does and for a young man to have such a weapon. Even then it could have been coincidental I suppose but then why would he come in to report it, except of course to put us off the scent and blame this man that he knew and knew that he wouldn't have an alibi.' Leonard was starting to warm to the idea.

'We should question him again sir.' David said.

'Yes and we will, but first I want to find out exactly who was at that party and if our Martin Baxter was there. It's not exactly a good time of day to find out but we must do what we can now then we can carry on later when everyone is at home if need be. Come on we have more work to do.'

David sighed and rose stiffly, it was looking like being a long day and he wondered if it would be another evening when he would miss reading Louise a bedtime story.

2.00pm Tuesday September 21st 1960

Martin was getting very stiff. It was cold in the alley, already he could hardly feel his hands or feet as the wind blew in mercilessly funnelled into the narrow space and he knew he had to move soon before he froze up. He staggered to his feet, trying to flex his stiff joints and he took another wistful look down the street to number twenty three then he turned and walked back up to the main road.

Well, the man had been in the house all morning, Martin figured so maybe another few hours wouldn't matter, they wouldn't have to anyway as he had to move. Already he had been seen a few times but no one had taken any notice, approached him or said anything. There was nothing else for it he just had to go and warm up, maybe get a bite to eat then return later and just hope that the man wouldn't have gone out in the meantime.

Before he knew it he had walked into the town centre and to the market hall, which was housed in a large extravagant grade two listed Victorian building and had some semblance of warmth to it. It had a high arched ceiling with a network of metal rods and everywhere was painted in different colours. The stalls on the ground floor were arranged in rows back to back and at every two or three there was a way through between them creating a maze of walkways for him to wander around. He walked upstairs to a balcony, which continued all around the four sides, and there were market stalls here as well. He lingered a while standing by the handrail looking down on the brightly coloured market stalls before going back down. In here he wouldn't be noticed and he wandered aimlessly around the stalls for a while which carried a wide range of goods. There was a newspaper stall that also sold magazines which was Martin's favourite. Here he would pause and glance through a few magazines that interested him knowing he wouldn't be bothered, not for a few minutes anyway. There were clothes stalls and people selling groceries, hardware and there were two butchers and a pet stall. Altogether it was an interesting place that would usually keep him occupied for some time.

This was a place he had been to many times before, entrance was free and he could be alone while in company of all the people going about their shopping. It was out of the wind and rain and offered him a safe haven to go to. No one knew him and he was careful not to strike up a conversation with anyone. It was quiet enough for him to have his own thoughts while busy enough to be of interest. The smell of toasting pyclets came to him and his tummy rumbled. Eventually he went to a cafe in one corner and he bought himself a cup of tea and a pyclet with what little money he had and thought through what to do next.

He could go home for a while but then he didn't know which or if either of his parents would be in and he didn't want to have an argument about where he had been and what he had or hadn't done. Also he couldn't be sure if the police had called and the trouble that would have caused him. So he stayed where he was wondering what time would be good to go back to the man's house. It crossed his mind to go back and hide in the garden, maybe then at least he would hear the man in some way or even see him through the kitchen window. Yes that was a good idea; he wondered why he hadn't thought of it earlier. Surely if the man was going out he would go to the kitchen first to make a drink or something? Whatever, it was a chance he was going to take, as he didn't want to wait in the street again just yet. He waited until he was fully warmed up and feeling as though he could go and then he got up and went back out into the cold day his hands thrust deep in his coat pockets.

Getting back into the garden had been quite easy and as far as he knew he had done so unobserved. It was sheltered here from the wind and when Martin pressed himself down under a large bush he was surprised at how warm it was as he settled himself in. He was sure he could not be seen from the house although his position only gave him a limited view into the kitchen. The curtains were still all drawn at the front and back of the house apart from the kitchen he had noted and there were no lights on or sounds to be heard. So it was a case once again of waiting it out. He settled himself down having decided to take a chance and wait here until it got a lot later and hoped that the man would show himself at the window.

5.00pm Tuesday September 21st 1960

Nathaniel woke refreshed and got up straight away. He stretched himself slowly, pulling his muscles and working them around to loosen up then completed his ablutions carefully and deliberately after all he still had some pride in himself and he liked to be clean as he always was especially before going out working which he intended to do tonight. Of course work to him was not like any other kind of job. His work was getting what he could where he could by any means he could. He looked at himself in the mirror and saw a man who was getting older. He wondered just how much longer he could sustain his life style especially without being caught. Sometime soon he knew he would have to stop, sell the house he was in and start to use that money plus the amount he had saved up to start a new life with. Soon it would have to be but not just yet, he could keep going for a little while longer. The thought of going off maybe to the coast and taking it easy appealed to him and there should be enough money to last him although a little more would not do any harm he thought.

For all his faults he still needed to feel good about himself although his looks didn't help and in fact he was very polite to anyone he found he had to talk to and he had empathy for a lot of people and animals, especially animals, well they couldn't talk back could they or hurt him, at least not emotionally. Times were when he would have tried harder to be a normal good citizen that was until he discovered that no one really cared about him or would give him anything, so gradually he turned more and more to crime and once he had murdered although that was really an accident there was no turning back. Keeping a low profile suited him well and the house was good enough for his needs. The house had been paid for a long time ago by his parents so he hadn't had to worry about a mortgage, which had been very useful when his father had died, and he was in a low paid job though even then it was hard to make ends meet, he found it quite ironic that he could get money so easily now while others had to work hard for it.

In the kitchen he set about making himself something to eat. He was wearing his pyjamas with a dressing gown over them. He never bothered with regular meals or to keep regular hours, he ate when he was hungry and slept when he was tired which was mostly in the day because he would be out most nights looking for somewhere to steal from or someone to rob. Now it was mostly just because he wanted to hit back at society for the life he had been forced to live for so long rather than a need for the money. It filled a need in him that couldn't be satisfied and he would keep on going for as long as he could, secure that there was a good stash of money for his old age. He didn't actually steal every night, often he was just sizing suitable places up and finding his way around, staking somewhere out or if he had taken something of value he would be going off to his fence to get rid of it or he would find a little job to keep him busy for a little while. So he fried himself what many would call a breakfast of eggs bacon and tomatoes with toast and a mug of tea and sat down at the table to eat it.

His fence was someone he had been going to for a long time. The man's name was Jacob Thompson. He was a small diminutive man with a totally bald head and wizened features. The kind of man nobody would ever notice or bother with and each time Nathanial went to him there would be the same shake of his head as though the item was worthless then a preamble to come up with a price which he paid for in cash. The system worked for both of them and neither of them got to know much about the other which also suited both of them.

He had a small shop on the outskirts of the town, which was fronted as a second hand shop, a fact that helped him to move some of the items that came to him. It was quite a small shop with items piled up everywhere with a pathway between them down to a desk at the back which Jacob sat behind. Behind him was a door to the rear area where he kept things he didn't want on show.

It had taken Nathanial quite a long time to find anyone like him and he had spent several evenings chatting to men in pubs before he got a lead on him. Even so the man was not easy to win over and Nathanial had to go there several times over a period of some months to get him to trust him.

Eventually a trust was made and now Nathanial took virtually everything there that was of any value to him. True he only got a small fraction of what the item was worth but it was still worth it to him to get rid of them and to get some money whatever the amount was.

Outside in the garden Martin could smell the food and his tummy rumbled although he had eaten at the cafe. How he wished he could have joined in with that instead of sitting out here, cold and hungry in spite of his snack in the market hall. At least it told him that the man was in the house, which was something, more than nothing, it was what Martin had wished for. He watched him cooking his food and sitting down to eat it. He obviously wasn't dressed so he wouldn't be going out for a little while yet at least which meant he had even longer to wait to gain access to the house if the man went out at all. What was more interesting was the fact that now Martin could see his face and would be able to recognise him again more easily in future and would be able to give the description to the police although they may guess that he had got this information after the murder.

Nathaniel washed his pots carefully when he had finished and put them away, quite unaware that he was being watched. He then returned upstairs and got dressed in the clothes he would wear for the night. They were sombre dark items, black thick twill trousers, a wool shirt with a thick fisherman's jumper over it then his black great coat together with his big black boots. A dark green trilby on his head and a warm dark blue scarf around his neck and over the bottom portion of his face completed his dress. He looked at himself in his wardrobe mirror; he knew no one would recognise him wearing these clothes.

There was still an important item he needed and he went to his walk in cupboard in the corner of his bedroom. It was full height before it went lower under the staircase that led up to the attic. In the far corner, he had taken out a panel of boards a long time ago then reworked them so they fitted very well and provided a perfect hidey hole for those items he wanted to keep secret. Here was where he kept the clothes he used for his hunting forays as he called his crime trips when he wasn't wearing them, a metal case filled with money and beside it his hunting knife in its brown leather sheath. He only kept the sheath to protect the knife and now he pulled it out and popped it into his pocket. He liked it like this so it was always handy to take out when he needed it. He had wiped it clean from killing the girl but he was aware that it was very difficult to remove all traces of blood from it especially as due to its age and use it was pitted in places although he was sure to always keep the edge very sharp. He also took the girl's handbag having searched it before to ensure there was nothing incriminating inside it ensuring his fingerprints did not get onto it by holding the strap in a handkerchief and dropping it into a paper bag.

Returning downstairs he checked that the kitchen was clear and the light was out which had been on as it was now 6.30 pm and getting dark outside. Then he left by the front door and out into the street. He walked on purposefully hoping to see the boy again while he was out who had witnessed the murder of the girl and if he did, he would make sure that he didn't cause any more trouble for him.

Martin was very pleased to see the man appear in the kitchen fully dressed in his hat and coat before leaving the room again. At least now he knew that he hadn't missed him going out. All he had to do now was make sure that he had definitely left the house. He hurried back out of the garden and down to the end of the alleyway and peered around to look down the street in time to see him disappearing around the far corner into the main road so now he was sure that he had gone.

Now his chance was here and it hadn't arrived soon enough. Martin hurried back down the alley and through the garden and went straight to the inside far corner of the house and looked up to see the window still slightly open above him. Spitting on his hands he grabbed hold of the drainpipe and began to shin up rather like when he had shinned up ropes at school. This was much harder work than he had anticipated though and half way up he was horrified to see one of the brackets holding the drainpipe to the wall rattle. He slowed his climb and tried to shin past it but his foot just caught it and it came free and then clattered to the ground below.

The pipe was now very loose and he was finding it hard to keep his balance and continue up. Carefully he inched his way upwards slowly until thankfully his fingers finally gripped the window lintel. It was rough stone and he was able to grip it easily enough although it hurt his hand. With an effort he inched just a little higher until he was able to rest a knee on the lintel and take some of the strain off the pipe. Now all he had to do was open the window. He got the fingers of his left hand under the bottom sash frame and pushed up, but it would not move. He began to panic thinking of the sash windows where he lived. One of those was very stiff and wouldn't move in either direction, was that why this window was slightly open all the while he wondered? There was no time to worry about that now he just had to get the window open somehow. Steadying him as best as he could he tried again using all his strength to push up. There was a loud creaking noise and it moved up an inch then stopped again. Martin couldn't bear the thought of having to go down again and force another way into the house so he tried again but to no effect. This was going to be difficult. He needed to use both his hands but the lintel was not very wide. With no choice, he hung on tight with his left hand then pulled himself over so that both his knees were balanced on the lintel and both hands were now gripping the bottom of the window frame. He jerked and heaved hard at the old wooden frame and was very relived to feel it go up, it stopped again after a few inches but now he was well balanced and with some more room to work his arms he tried again and eventually the window was open just wide enough for him to gain access into the room.

He dropped inside and looked around, it was quite dark so he was pleased he had brought his torch with him, he daren't turn the light on in case someone noticed. The torch gave just enough light without being too obvious from outside. The room was quite large and virtually empty, just a low long cupboard sat against the far wall, which he quickly found to be empty. The question was where would he find any evidence? This had been on his mind since he had traced the man back here and he had given quite some thought as to where he would hide anything such as the girl's handbag. It would have to be out of sight of course and probably somewhere that you would not normally think of, but where? There was only one way to find out and Martin started straight away by checking quickly around the rest of the room before leaving and going out onto the landing, this ran down to another room on the left into which Martin entered. This had a lot more in it. A bed, a wardrobe, a dressing table with a pot bowl and jug on it and in a corner a small table under a window with a lamp on it which looked like it was used for writing on. It had a whiskey bottle and a glass on it. There was a lot to look through and Martin hurriedly got to work but after an extensive search, he found nothing. He wasn't too worried about the time as he expected the man to be out for quite a while. He made sure he put everything back exactly as he had found it just in case he didn't find it today and had to come back again when he could for a second try. However, he couldn't take too long and he hurried back to the other bedroom where again he found nothing after having searched through the few items of furniture that there were. He looked under the bedclothes, behind pictures and checked under the cupboards in case he had secured it there with tape but he couldn't find anything to help him.

He then went into a small third bedroom down the landing and although he searched carefully and checked the walls and floorboards for any hiding holes, he came out again empty handed.

Further along the landing he found a doorway that led to stairs going up to a small attic. This he thought was really promising. It was dusty and musty up there with mostly junk and cardboard boxes strewn around. Sighing he started work and searched through every item. He could see reasonably well with the light from a skylight although he used his torch as well but again after a lengthy search he found nothing. Going down stairs to the ground floor was no better; he went from room to room and did not find anything to implement the man in the murder anywhere. He kept on thinking where he would hide anything but all such places drew a blank. What interested him as well was the fact that he didn't find anything to identify the man either. There were no photographs, no diary, no paperwork or information anywhere that gave his name or any other kind of information about him, which he thought was rather strange. The man was obviously very secretive and careful to hide his identity in every way. What if he was a serial killer as he had read about, wouldn't he want to keep some mementoes or stash anything he got? And then what of the murder weapon, the knife, surely he would want to keep that hidden away somewhere.

He went back upstairs thinking he would have to give up after all and get out of the house the same way he had got in before the man came back. On the landing he decided to take one more quick look in the main bedroom as that was where he would hide anything important to keep it close to him. Walking in he stopped and looked around carefully, noting everything in the room. Most things and places he had already searched even the walk in cupboard in the corner; absently he walked over to it again, opened the door and walked in. The space was about five feet deep and three feet wide going lower as it went in with the staircase going above to the attic. There were clothes hanging up and a case on the floor, which he had already searched, however he pulled it out into the room and checked around the space. As he moved some boxes about there came a creak from the floorboards and looking down he could see where the boards didn't quite meet in the far corner. Closer inspection revealed boards that didn't quite fit at the bottom of the wall. Bending down he took out the penknife he had brought with him and prised away at a gap between the boards. He found that two lengths of board came away quite easy and to his delight he spied inside a large metal box beside which disappointingly was a sheaf for a long knife but no knife.

The metal box was surprisingly heavy as he pulled it out and laid it on the floor before opening the lid. He could hardly believe his eyes at what he found inside; there were bank notes, hundreds of them all neatly stacked in bundles. He lifted a few out and wondered just how much money there was in the box? He thought that there must be thousands of pounds. He sat back on the floor and wondered what to do next. He could just run off with the money, there was surely enough there for him to build a new life with which was very tempting but then the man would get away with murder and it would be theft. It was agonising for him to decide but then he reached back in and separated out a twenty pound note. That would pay for the trouble he had taken so far he thought and the man would never miss it. Quickly he pocketed it.

Seeing the money had thrown his mind but now he just sat and stared at the empty knife sheaf. The man had gone out and obviously had taken the knife with him. Was he off to do another murder? Martin suddenly panicked. He had spent all this time searching while the man was out there contemplating God only knew what. He had to go out there after him, see if he could possibly find him and stop him if he could. Hurriedly he put everything back as it had been and made again for the window in the back bedroom. He eased himself out, sat on the lintel, and reached over for the drainpipe. It was further than he thought and was awkward to reach from this angle and he had to shuffle over to get a hand onto it. Then he swung himself out and grabbed the drainpipe with both hands. The pipe made a complaining groan and shifted in his hands. He gripped tight with his knees and feet and reached back up to pull the window down to where it was when he arrived which it did a lot easier than being pushed up then gradually he shinned down to the ground taking care not to disturb the pipe any more than he had to.

He hurried through the garden ensuring that he closed the gate, into the alley and out into the street. He turned left immediately as he had seen the man turn to go onto the main road. At the junction the next decision was easy, to head into town. As he hurried along, he realised that from here the man could be anywhere, well not anywhere, he would avoid the busy areas and the town centre, he would probably be on side streets or in quiet areas where he could work in peace. Martin racked his brains for suitable places to look; focussing on those close by as he hurried on.

* * *

Nathanial had decided that tonight he would go a little further out of town to an area he had checked up on some time ago and he set off at a brisk pace. He usually walked and only took a bus or a train on rare occasions, lessoning the chances of him being identified. The handbag he had put into a paper bag he dropped into a waste bin well away from his house.

The houses he was targeting were in a suburban area and were mostly detached houses with a few semi detached thrown in here and there. These areas usually had richer picking than the area he lived in. It was to the detached houses he looked at, as these would be easier for him to get in without being noticed. It was a quiet area and he had no trouble getting there unobserved, well not noticed by anyone anyway. He slowed down in the street he was interested in and looked closely at each house as he walked past. He had been here before as he often did when looking for a new target, walking round at different times, noting who was in, what cars and bikes were around and at what times. He had noted who lived in several of the houses and which ones had cars in the drives. Now a particular house came up and he smiled to see that there was no car in the drive tonight although he had seen one there a few times before. There were no lights on and so he looked all around to ensure he was not being watched and slipped through the front garden gate, up the path and through another gate that led to the back garden and he hurried up to the side of the house. There were no sounds coming from the house and he carefully walked all around looking in all the windows as he went. Finally he was as sure as he could be that the house was empty. As it was in an up market urban area and he sure that there would be some rich pickings inside.

He walked back a few feet into the garden and looked at all the windows and doors and looked up to see if an upstairs window was open. There wasn't but that didn't trouble him. He returned to the kitchen door that was at the back of the house. The garden was a decent size and there were trees and high hedges all around that hid him from any prying eyes. The door had small glass windows on the top half and was locked, there was no sign of a key in the lock or hidden under the mat or anywhere else he could find so Nathanial went to the window. This window was also divided up into smaller panes and using his well padded elbow he smashed one closest to the window catch. It was then easy enough to reach in and open the window.

He climbed in over the sink and had a quick check around the room. Finding nothing of any interest he moved on through a door into a hallway. This led to the front door and the stairs and there were two doors leading to rooms. The first one was being used as a dining room and apart from some china there was nothing of any value, he took a bag from a pocket he had brought with him and put what he knew to be a couple of good pieces in it and then undeterred he went on into the next room, the lounge. Here were a few things he fancied, a gold cigarette lighter, some silver items in a glass cupboard and then in a drawer he found a wallet, looking inside there was quite a few pounds in notes all of which he pocketed. The bigger items he found of interest went into his bag. Upstairs he found more money in a box hidden under a bed and a few items of jewellery that he knew he could pass on quite easily. Having got what he could he returned downstairs and helped himself to a whiskey bottle which he popped in his bag before going back to the kitchen. He was sure he had left no signs of himself being there having worn gloves throughout, no hairs could have fallen from under his hat and there were no other signs left that could help the police detect him. He then climbed back up onto the sink and out of the window. Half way out something caught on a piece of broken glass. Nathanial gave no thought to it thinking it was just rather a tight fit, however his coat had caught and a piece had ripped off and stayed attached to the fragment of broken glass. Nimbly he jumped down to the ground and made his way back to the side of the house. Then looking carefully into the street and seeing no one around he walked off briskly away and back towards town.

7.30pm Tuesday September 21st 1960

Josephine had spent the afternoon musing around the warehouse that had yielded nothing of any use. There was only rubbish scattered around and also outside around the Industrial Estate. It covered a big area and there were businesses of all types. People had come and gone during the day, workers got on with their jobs and no one seemed to notice her except for one young man who was busy bringing timber out of a building and loading it onto a lorry. He kept on looking across at her until she felt uneasy and walked away. Some of the buildings had rubbish piled up at the rear, pieces of wood from a joinery shop, metal from another business. There were quite a lot of things but Josephine did not find anything of any use to her at all apart from a rubbish bin. Here she found a half drunk bottle of lemonade that turned out to be flat and a half eaten sandwich, which she ate. She did find a piece of tarpaulin though and some cardboard boxes that she took back to the den she had built to improve it.

Mr Henderson was very concerned. How could she have run off like that he thought. Would she come back? Would she report him for going to see her? But then how could she, after all he was her care worker and would have access to her. It would depend on what she said when and if she returned. What was he to do now. He sat at his desk deep in thought. He could just leave it and wait until the morning he supposed but what if she came back before then. He would want to be there to see how she was and what she was indeed prepared to say. He knew he had been a bit forward with her, well more than a bit. It was definitely a quandary to be in. Then he wondered what she would have taken with her and surreptitiously he hurried back down the corridors to her room and going inside closed the door.

He looked around and opened the wardrobe doors and checked the drawers. Finding nothing confirmed his suspicions that she had gone not intending to return. He wasn't sure whether this was a good thing or not? Had she really gone because of him? He couldn't rule that out in fact it seemed the most logical answer although he never intended to come down on her that hard and would never have hurt her but she evidently didn't see it like that.

So what was he to do? Raise the alarm or wait? After some thought he thought it best to leave it until the morning and let someone else make the discovery. Yes that would be best, keep himself out of it as much as possible and be surprised when he was told of her disappearance then just hope she would not be found. Of course if she was then that could cause complications for him. Well he would just have to deny anything she said and carry on as normal and hope for the best.

By early evening Josephine had been all around the Estate and arrived back to where she started from and searched around among the cardboard boxes and rubbish and found a few more pieces to make her den more comfortable which she did and where she then sat down on the cardboard boxes on the concrete floor again. There seemed to be only one way for her to be able to move on, she needed some money and again there was only one way for her to get some, she would have to steal it. Not at all what she wanted to do and she cursed Mr Henderson for putting her in this situation. Getting some work would be hard to do and with no address to give and the way she looked she ruled that out as a possibility. Stealing was the only way for her at the moment. She didn't expect it would be that hard. After all, she had been in several homes and met many people who stole from time to time and she had picked up quite a few tips from them.

The shops would have closed ages ago and the streets should be a quite empty by now she thought so it was a good time for her to move on and see what she could find. She checked her pockets and rucksack to see what she had that would be useful; there was the nearly empty bottle of water, a few clothes, a small bag with soap and other toiletries inside, a dark flat cap which she put on, a small torch with half used up batteries and then yes it was there, a penknife with several tools on which she had received as a present last Christmas from who she couldn't remember. That would be useful and she popped it into her trousers pocket to keep it handy. There was nothing much else that could be of any use so she shouldered her rucksack and started of purposefully for the shops that she had walked past earlier.

It wasn't long before she came to the row of small shops on a main road that was surprisingly quiet. As she approached she slowed her steps and looked all around her carefully but did not see anyone around so she carried on and stopped outside the first shop. It was a general store with lots of things in the window she wished she could have; sweets, cakes, and all manner of tasty things if she could just get inside. She walked along and looked in the windows of the other shops, the next one was a butchers which may have been interesting but the shelves were all bare, the next and last one was a toy shop with nothing of any use on show. The only interesting thing was an alleyway between the toy shop and the butchers and after looking round very carefully again to make sure no one was watching she crept in and walked quietly down to the end where she found two tall gates that were angled away at forty five degrees to give access to the rear of both buildings from the alley. One obviously led off into the back yard of the butchers. The other one she scrambled up and grasped the top and pulled herself up to look over. There was the back yard of the toy shop and a paved path to another gate that would lead to the rear of the general store. There were no lights from any of the buildings windows, which was good but she was still not sure if anyone was in the upper floors or not so very carefully she climbed over the gate and dropped down to the other side.

It was dark on this side of the buildings with no lights from anywhere as she carefully made her way to the next gate looking in the windows of the toy as she went which were closed up and dark and she pulled herself up the gate and after checking all was well she climbed over. The back of the next shop revealed a wooden door and a window to the side, which appeared to open into a small kitchen area. Looking around the yard she could see that the area was unkempt with weeds and bushes growing everywhere and there were also a few old cardboard boxes stacked up and some rubbish.

The door was locked which was to be expected and it looked a solid door to break. The window looked more promising however and she looked around for a brick or something to smash the glass but then she remembered the penknife in her pocket. She took it out and went back to the window. It was a sash window and she could see the catch easily on the other side. Opening the longest blade she inserted it between the windows and pushed against the catch. It didn't move and she suspected that it had not been opened for some time. She put both hands to it and pushed as hard as she could. To her delight it moved and eventually she was able to move it all the way across. She put her knife back in her trousers pocket and getting her fingers under the rim of the bottom half of the window frame she pushed up. Nothing happened the window was still tight shut. Desperately she pushed and pushed but it was no use the window was stuck fast possibly from layers of paint.

She stopped and rubbed her hands then looked around for anything she could use to prise it open with. There was all manner of junk items in the yard and she searched around as best as she could in the dim light only daring to use her torch a little in case it was seen. Nothing much cropped up, there was a brick end and she considered using it for a moment but she didn't want to make that much noise. There didn't seem to be anything and she was about to give up when something flashed in the undergrowth. Going closer she could see it was a metal bar about two feet long, about three inches wide and quite thin. She dragged it out and hefted it, yes it seemed just right for the job. Back at the window she pushed the end of the bar under the window and using the ledge as a fulcrum she heaved on the bar. There was a loud screech as the window opened a couple of inches, which made her stop especially as a dog started barking from a house down the street. She waited anxiously listening carefully. Eventually the dog stopped barking and silence returned. Wedging the bar in the window again she pushed on it and the window moved again, this time not squealing quite so loud. Just one more push, she thought then she could get in. The last push gave a loud squeal and she dropped the bar in shock, which clanged onto the ground. Again the dog started barking and Josephine stood very still hardly daring to breath.

* * *

Nathaniel was in no hurry to get home tonight, he strolled around going past the Industrial Estate and peered in a few windows and checked for what might have been left outside the buildings. He tried a few doors but decided not to stay long, after all some of them had security companies make patrols from time to time and he did not want to be caught by one of them. He started back to the town and as he walked along the streets became closer together, more shops appeared and it was these he was interested in. Most had little if any security and even that would normally not cause him any bother. He kept away from the town centre and walked around the outside perimeter of the Arboretum nearest the town, which was normally quiet apart from the occasional lady of the night who he avoided when spotted.

It was when he came across a short row of shops when he heard a dog barking and then a noise that he recognised, a noise he had made himself on occasions. Intrigued he hurried his steps and checked all around to make sure there was no one about to see him. The shops were right in front of him and as he got up to them there came another louder noise. Thinking that there may be something of advantage to him he decided to take a look. He took great care, found the alleyway and made his way down it to the rear of the shops.

Josephine started to breathe again as the dog stopped barking and she hurriedly climbed through the window deciding that it was now or never before her nerve broke. She climbed over the sink in front of the window and into the tiny kitchen, which was obviously just for making tea or a small snack. Ignoring the possibilities there she then sneaked into the next room opening the door carefully. Now she was in the main shop, which had another door to her right, and one to her left. She tried the left one first and found a staircase going up, leaving that door open she went across to the other door, which she opened. This was a stockroom with shelves and boxes of all sizes; some large ones were on the floor containing all kinds of items. Having looked around inside she went back into the main shop to see what was there; she could always go back to the stockroom if she wanted to. The shelves here had many items of use and she took her rucksack off and crammed inside it, two bottles of orange drink, tins of beans, sardines and spam, a small loaf of bread followed and then some sweets. She crammed other items in until her rucksack was full. Putting it back on she checked the till but soon saw that the drawer was open and that the till was empty.

She turned to go and as she reached the door to the kitchen she heard a noise coming from the rear of the building. Again she froze, horrified that someone was going to catch her in the act. A noise came again and she realised that someone was coming in through the window the same way as she had. She looked around hurriedly, where could she hide? The shop had nowhere suitable so she quietly hurried into the storeroom, thankful for leaving the door open and she crouched down behind the stacked cardboard boxes on the floor. She was only just in time as she heard someone enter the shop from the kitchen. She could hear the footsteps of whoever it was walking into the shop and she risked a quick peep over the boxes. She saw the back of a tall man wearing a thick overcoat and trilby hat as he went to the counter and the till. Josephine ducked down again fearful of what to do; surely he would come in the storeroom and catch her. She tried to stop her breathing in case he heard her as she listened to him walk around. Then his footsteps started back towards her and she heard him stop in the doorway. He stayed still for what seemed like a lifetime as her heart raced then to her relief she heard him back away and go to the other door leading upstairs. Again she was glad that she had also left that door open, maybe he would go up there so she could get out.

It was some moments later that she heard him doing that very thing and she rose and crept out back into the shop. The man's footsteps could now be heard as he walked around upstairs and she fled out of the shop into the kitchen and straight for the window. In her rush she didn't bother about how much noise she made and as she scrambled up over the sink to the window she knocked a cup off the drainer, which smashed loudly on the floor. Panicking now she hurried to get out and in her haste got a strap of her rucksack caught on the window catch. She had to back off and throw it out the window before climbing through herself.

Nathaniel heard the noise and hurried back downstairs. He knew from the sounds and the signs that someone had broken into the shop and he was interested to find out who it was and whether he could benefit from it. Seeing the open door to the upstairs and nothing to alert him in the stockroom he had assumed that whoever it was had gone upstairs, now he wished he had checked the stockroom properly first. He came crashing down the stairs, into the shop and on into the kitchen. There he could see Josephine almost out of the window and struggling to get out. Then she was gone like a flash and he was after her. He wanted to know who it was and whether she had seen enough of him to identify him. He had to abandon his bag of stolen items as he would never manage it with them but wasn't too worried; after all he could always come back for them. Clambering through the window he was not a nimble as she was or as small and he wasted valuable seconds wrestling himself out through the small gap, which is all the window would allow itself to open.

Josephine had quickly grabbed her rucksack, shrugged it on and ran off as fast as she could, fear spurring her on. She didn't know how she got over the first gate it was all such a blur then she was across the yard and climbing over the second one. Behind her she could hear the man coming after her swearing as he got hampered at the window. Another thing she was thankful for was that it hadn't fully opened and was jammed part way up which would make it difficult for the man to get through quickly.

As her hands reached the top of the gate she felt his hands close around her left ankle and she screamed as she fought to get free. Fear and surprise at being caught so quickly made her heart race such was her fright that she kicked out hard with her other foot and must have struck him because she heard a grunt and suddenly she was free and up over the gate. She dropped down and ran hard up the alleyway to the sounds of the man climbing over the gate and then she was out in the street. All she could think of now was getting away and the best place she could think of to lose him was in the Arboretum, which was just a short way along the main road and up a short side street. She was sure that she could lose him amongst all the trees and over the hills in the park if she could just keep well in front of him. She ran on not daring to look behind her. The rucksack was now heavy and uncomfortable and hampered her speed but she was not going to leave it behind and she ran on determinedly.

Nathaniel cursed as Josephine's foot kicked his hand, which held him up for a few seconds before he too was up and over the gate and running down the alleyway. What concerned him now was whether the girl had seen his face or had any other way of identifying him. He had to catch her and find out and then, well he would deal with her. Angrily he surged on after her his feet pounding on the paving.

Josephine was quite fit, she had never eaten enough to get fat and she walked a lot, also she ran often and liked to keep herself fit in case of any occasion when she needed to be so and now here was such an occasion. Pumping her arms she kept up a relentless steady fast rhythm as she ran down the road.

Nathaniel was finding it hard to keep up; he was older, not so fit as the girl although he was fit enough as he liked to be for his lifestyle. However he had stamina and he kept on going following the girl along the main road then up a side street. He could see where they were heading and knew he would have to be good to catch her once they got to the park. There were several entrances and many places where she could hide and avoid him if he lost sight of her. He hurried on thinking hard, the few extra items he had in his pockets from the house hampering him.

Josephine was breathing more heavily as she entered the park. She had come from the street into the orangery, which was at the end of the street, which was in fact a cul-de-sac. The orangery was quite a long building but narrow and she went straight across and out an exit into the park where she turned right and ran on trying to get bushes and trees in between her and her pursuer.

Nathaniel knew he could not outrun her in a straight race so he had to use cunning if he was to catch her. As he came out of the orangery he saw her disappearing around a bend and he went straight on through the trees. Unknown to Josephine Nathaniel now knew the park very well indeed and he knew where all the paths led.

10.00pm Tuesday September 21st 1960

Martin was unsure which way to go. Where would Nathaniel be off to tonight he kept wondering? There was no way of knowing; all he could do was walk around and hope that the man had been doing the same thing for a while. It occurred to him to look around where there were businesses or shops that he might rob or that might be places where he could find people to mug or even just to weigh up for the future. However after a lot of searching there had been no sign of him. Martin's wanderings brought him around close to home and he thought of going back there for a sleep. Without thinking his feet took him that way which meant him crossing through the Arboretum from where he now was.

* * *

Josephine was getting tired and she stopped under a big tree and looked around panting and trying to get her breath back. There was no sound or sight of the man and she wondered if she had lost him or whether was he was somewhere close by waiting for her to show? She didn't have many choices; she could either stay here and hide somewhere or carry on out of the park and back to the Industrial Estate building that she had been using to shelter in. She felt she would be safer in the building on the Estate so she carried on, walking quickly and looking all about her at the same time. The path she had chosen wound around the park to the top entrance, which she realised was in the opposite direction to which she needed to go. The best way from where she was would be to leave the path and run over the hills in the park and through the trees to the far entrance, which is what she started to do.

Nathaniel kept on running, keeping his profile off the tops of the hills. He looked from side to side as he hurried on, sure that his path would cross hers very soon and then he would pounce. The park was dark and quiet, the only sounds being the wind rustling the leaves through the trees. Even that was not a lot as the wind had died down to a slight breeze. The sky was still dark with threatening rain clouds only allowing glimpses of the moon to give some light and it was peaceful and lonely in the park.

Josephine had to stop running as she was developing a stitch in her side but kept on walking fast and her path took her through the trees and shrubberies and out over open areas, rather than walk around them which would extend her time here and her chances of being caught she just ran, holding her side and hoping not to be seen. She kept hoping she would meet other people who she could join for protection but the park was empty. There was not far to go now and she would be back out into the streets and she hurried her pace. There was just one other copse of trees to go through and then she should be able to see the gate. She entered cautiously then stepped out running again through the trees.

Nathanial heard a noise as he ran over to his right and he steered towards it hopeful that it was the girl and not someone or something else. He was getting out of breath and knew he would have to stop soon which he did beside a big oak tree. Here he leaned against the bark and waited for his breathing to return to normal. If he had lost the girl then he had, there was nothing more he could do, at least for the moment. So it was with a surprise that he heard someone running up towards him. Carefully he looked around the tree trying to see who it was. Then there she was running virtually towards him. All he had to do now was move a little way to another tree close by and then she would be within range of him as she came past.

Josephine was sure now that she must have lost him, she had been running hard and she doubted if an older person would have been able to keep up with her even though she was carrying a heavy rucksack. Her breathing was becoming hard and laboured and she would have to stop soon for a rest. She kept on now, hoping to reach the entrance before she stopped and she was slowing down, also her attention was waning with the effort of running. Then suddenly it happened, a hand grasped her shoulder and held her in an iron grip. Josephine screamed and tried to turn round but the grip was too tight and the man was close up behind her holding her in place.

'Just take it easy now and you will be all right.' His voice was throaty in her ear, the knife flashed close to her face and she stopped struggling.

'What do you want?' She asked fearful of the answer.

'For a start we will see what's in your rucksack.'

He took hold of one of the straps and pulled it off her shoulder.

'There is nothing of value, I need it, get off me.'

Josephine was not going to lose all her possessions that easily and she screamed again, twisting and turning, trying to get free. Together they struggled and Nathanial began to press down on Josephine forcing her to the ground.

'We will soon see what you have of value.' Nathanial sneered.

When she fell he was on top of her and turned her over onto her front pulling again at the straps of her rucksack while holding her down with his weight as she screamed for help. Nathanial slapped her and she stopped.

Martin heard the scream, it had come from over on his left and he turned instinctively towards the sound. He started to run with mixed thoughts, maybe it was Nathanial at his dirty work again and he had by chance happened across him at the right time although if it was him he hoped to be in time to stop anything really bad happening although of course it could be anyone. As he ran he heard a second scream and ran faster towards the sound not knowing what he would find or what he would do when he got there.

He knew he was close and that the scream had come from a bank of trees and it was there he ran as fast as he could. As he ran into the trees he could see a dark shape further in of a man crouched over someone on the ground. It was obvious to him immediately that it was Nathanial, the clothes and the shape left him in no doubt bringing memories back of the last time he had seen him.

Without stopping he ran on and started shouting at the top of his voice, 'Hey you, stop.' Then he suddenly thought to say, 'Come on men let's get him.'

Nathanial was shocked and stopped what he was doing. The thought of being attacked by several men frightened him and he rose to his feet shoving Josephine to one side and losing hold of the rucksack. Without even a backward glance he ran off through the trees towards the park exit.

Martin was extremely relieved, as he would not have known what to do if Nathanial had not run off and he thanked his lucky stars for thinking of his ploy. He now ran to what he could see was a girl still lying on the ground.

Josephine was trying to get her rucksack back on while scrambling up into a sitting position tears streaming down her face, unable to do much because of the shock of what had just happened.

Martin knelt down beside her and asked, 'Are you all right?'

'I, I think so,' Came her slow reply. Thank you, he was trying to steal my things.'

'I know, I saw him.' Martin said lamely. He crouched down and put a hand on her arm to steady her and give comfort, 'Can you stand?'

'Yes, I'm ok.' Josephine shrugged his hand off and staggered clumsily to her feet. Unsteady as she was Martin held an arm again to keep her upright. This time she didn't shrug him off.

'We need to get out of here.' Martin said, looking round, 'We don't want him to realise that I am on my own and have him come back.'

Josephine looked at him shocked, 'Yes, yes of course,' She looked around nervously before pulling free and started to walk off. Martin ran after her and stopped her.

'Maybe we should go a different way, that is the direction he went.'

She stopped and looked around then at Martin, 'Oh, would you walk with me to the bottom gates please I don't want to meet him again?'

'Of course, yes, wherever, I have nowhere special to go.' Martin felt sorry for the girl and anger at Nathanial for attacking her but also very pleased indeed that he had managed to stop him going further with her and he kept close beside her as they walked along.

'How do you mean, you have nowhere to go?' Josephine asked looking at her protector.

'It's a long story, but home life is not so good and I have nowhere else to go. Listen you ought to report that man to the police but I can walk you home first if you like and I will talk to your parents.'

Josephine stopped and turned to face him, 'I have nowhere to go either, except,' She paused and wondered if she could trust this stranger, 'Except where I have a den at the moment. I have no home to go to or any parents either.' The words came out in a rush.

Martin stared at her and saw a lonely frightened girl with tangled dirty curly hair that ran about her shoulders a scruffy dirty jacket over a thick jumper together with dark practical trousers and shoes that needed mending but underneath it all he also saw a pretty girl with big blue eyes and a generous smile, a slim figure that would put many girls to shame. He then realised that she was nursing her left hand.

'Hey, what's wrong with your hand?'

She looked down and said, 'That man twisted my wrist when he tried to take my things.'

'Let's have a look,' Martin said gently taking her hand and turning it over. Josephine winced and he said, 'It is certainly bruised, you need to bathe it in cold water, maybe strap it up.'

'I only have a little water with me.'

Martin looked around and said, 'Look the Orangery is just over there and there is a tap, come on I will help you.'

The orangery was convenient also being one of the entrance ways to the park they could get out easily if they had to and Josephine resigned herself to being helped, at least for the time being and allowed herself to be led along.

While they walked Martin asked her name and gave her his and he explained that he lived close by but couldn't really bear being at home much.

'That is odd as I never had a home really to live in.' Josephine said in return.

'Oh, I'm sorry."

'No need to be, I have had several foster parents but nothing worked out for me.'

'But surely you have somewhere to go?' Martin sad concerned for her.

Josephine looked down as they walked along, 'I was in a care home, but I escaped.'

'Escaped!'

'Look it's a long story but there was someone there I didn't like, that I had to get away from.' Josephine kept her head down as she walked along.

Martin thought for a moment, 'So you really have nowhere to go now?'

'Only a place that I have found but I can't stay there long.'

'Well I will go there with you, make sure you get there safely.'

Josephine nodded her thanks. She was still not quite sure of this boy but he seemed genuine and at the moment she needed his help.

At the Orangery Martin led her to the tap and she allowed him to bathe her hand carefully, 'What we need now is something to strap it up with,' He said.

Josephine pulled her rucksack closer with her other hand and tried to open the straps.

'Here, let me do that.' He took her rucksack off her and opened it up.

'There is a thin towel in there, maybe you could pull a strip off it to use.'

Martin sat her down on a bench and got busy with his knife to take a strip from the towel then bound up her hand and wrist.

'I was really worried when I first saw you, I thought that murderer may have killed you.'

Josephine pulled back fear in her face, 'Murderer! What, you know him?'

Martin hesitated then said, 'No, I don't actually know him but I know of him.' He then sat back and poured out the whole story of him seeing the other girl being killed and all that had happened up to now, really pleased to have someone to tell it to.

'Wow, that is quite a story, he really needs sorting out.'

'Yes he does and you should report him attacking you.'

Josephine wasn't so sure, 'If I do that they will take me back to the care home.'

'Ah, and that would be bad?'

'Very. They don't look out for me very well, I am too much trouble for them and then there is Mr Henderson.'

'What about Mr Henderson?'

Josephine looked at Martin, then looked down, 'Well you know. He is the one I had to get away from.'

Martin was shocked, 'What you don't mean that he has assaulted you?'

'Not yet, well not exactly but there's no way I am going back there to see if he does.'

'Have you reported it?'

'I have mentioned it yes, but no one believes me and I have no proof.'

Martin said nothing.

'So you see I can't report that man, I can't identify him anyway apart from his clothes, there is nothing I can do about it.'

'Yes I see, and I need proof to show the police in order to get him.'

'What kind of proof?'

'Well anything really, the knife would be good. I am sure they will be able to match it to the murder and there will be his fingerprints on it. But then maybe I could get something else, you know the girl's handbag or something, anything to convince the police of what I have told them. '

'Yes the knife would be good? It looked quite an evil weapon.' Josephine said quietly, 'That I did see and can identify.'

'Yes it is quite a knife,' Seeing Josephine's face, he quickly continued, 'I would not have let him hurt you and I mean to get him arrested no matter what.'

Josephine thought for a moment before saying, 'What if he has killed others?'

'That has crossed my mind in which case there could be other evidence I could get but so far I haven't found any.'

'It sounded really dangerous breaking into his house, you must be very brave.'

Martin shook his head, 'No not at all, it just seems the right thing to do and I can't really go back on it now.'

Josephine smiled, 'Thanks but that is going to be rather difficult isn't it, especially on your own?'

'I know but there is no one else to help me.' Martin looked down at his hands.

'I will help you.'

Martin suddenly looked up, 'What, no you can't take the risk.'

'What, you think I am a girl and useless too?'

Martin shook his head, 'No, not at all, I just want to protect you and help you.'

'Well you have so far and very well too, so now I will help you and as you know I have nothing else to do. So what do we do first?'

Martin smiled, thankful for having her with him it would be so good to have someone to share all this with, 'We go to your hideout and rest up for a while, then we can go back to his house and see what we can do about getting in again, hopefully when he has left some evidence. It would be great if he went out and left the knife for me to find.'

Josie just nodded in agreement and together they stood up and set off.

'So you are all alone then?' Martin asked as they walked along side by side.

Josephine stared to talk, for some strange reason she felt that she could talk to this boy who she had only just met better than any of the care workers she had ever known, 'Yes, I have been for years, both my parents were killed in a car accident and no one in the family wanted me not that there were many to choose from anyway.'

'I'm sorry to hear that,' Martin replied while wondering if he would have been any better off in her circumstances.

'So I was put into care and have been passed around ever since.'

'How could that be, I would have thought any family would want you.'

Josephine smiled and stopped to look closely at him, 'Thank you but that 's not how it worked out. I was placed with a family then other family's but they never wanted me with them for long.' She waved her hand to stop his interruption, 'I suppose I was too hard to handle, after all losing your parents is a big deal no matter how old you are. There was only one couple that really wanted me and they were very kind, I would have stayed with them but then the wife became ill and he couldn't look after me anymore. All the others thought I was uncontrollable, rowdy, always in trouble and the constant arguments so they always sent me back to a care home and that's where I was before running away.'

'That sounds really bad, I am sorry you had all that happen to you.'

'You just have to get on, although I am not sure how yet. But what about you though, you don't seem very happy either?'

'Ah well my story is a bit different to yours. I have both my parents but you wouldn't want them. My dad is a bit of a lout, often drunk, always angry. He steals things too and has been arrested for it before. I never have been able to get on with him and I just try to keep out of his way as much as I can. He shouts at mum too but then she is not much better really, she lives in her own world and has no time for me. We don't have much money, in fact I don't have any really and I haven't been able to find a job I can do or want to do. With no qualifications it is difficult, there is only manual labour, which I can't do or shop work, which I can't stand. My last job was all right at a factory packing sweets but things have changed there and they don't need me any longer.'

'Sounds like I should be sorry for you.'

Martin laughed, 'Yes, having parents isn't always a good thing.'

They talked on and by the time they arrived at the building on the Industrial Estate they knew an awful lot more about each other.

* * *

Nathanial walked around the park checking behind him occasionally. He thought of the bag of items he had left at the shop and decided he ought to go back for them. When they were found it would be another link back to him. He also checked the items he had put in his pockets. Some money, a gold cigarette lighter and a couple of small silver ornaments.

He worked his way back around to the shops still shocked by what had happened and entered the alleyway from the deserted street. At the gates he easily climbed over the first one and made his way to the second. Here he stopped and listened, what had he heard? Something had alerted his keen senses and he strained to hear any sound. Then he heard it, voices talking, they were coming from the shop, they were faint

96

but there. He took a chance and pulled himself to the top of the gate and peered over. He could see that the door to the shop was now open, the light was on and there were at least two people inside talking. That was enough for him and he dropped down again and quickly headed back and out into the street. He had to move off fast now as he suspected that the police would have been called and could be here at any moment. He wondered how anyone could have got there so fast? There was no one living upstairs. Whoever had got there must have been close by and the noises no doubt had alerted them. He thought for a few moments about the bag he had left. Was there anything in it that could lead the police back to him? He doubted it. It was only an old cloth bag he had found recently in a waste bin that he had taken for that very purpose. The only things inside it were those taken from the house and his fingerprints weren't on them so he relaxed and set off for home.

* * *

David was late getting home, it had been a long slog of a day what with trying to get further on the murder case and he was still following up on the spate of burglaries and muggings that had sprung up again, a case that he had been working on. It was every so often and he wondered if it was all down to the same man. He had no proof but they all seemed similar in various ways but he still couldn't decide for sure or put a name to them.

Judith was waiting for him when he arrived and was sorry he hadn't managed to get home earlier.

'Louise missed, you, she even asked for you as daddy.' Judith smiled, recalling her daughters first request for her father.

David was disappointed, 'Oh dear I always miss the good things. I will just take a quick peek.'

Quietly he went up to her bedroom and slipped up to her cot. She looked very peaceful lying there with the toys hanging above her and he planted a kiss on her forehead before going back downstairs.

After dinner he sank down into an armchair with a glass of wine and chatted to Judith. He didn't normally discuss cases with her and kept his business life separate but on this occasion he mentioned the murder and how Martin had come up with the murderers address.

'It does sound strange that this lad should do that.' Judith commented.

'That's what we think. Maybe it is as he said although when we visited the man we didn't find anything, but then maybe he just trying to set him up or even just an address he knew to throw us of the scent.'

Judith folded her legs under her on the settee and wrapped her hands around a coffee mug, 'But why would he do that, he must have a reason.'

David thought for a moment, 'Yes he must. This man would have had to have wronged him quite seriously for that and no reason has appeared yet. if it was that, we still have a lot to sort out.'

'Well I am sure you will sort it out.' Judith said and began to relate to him the things she had done with Louise that day.

David kept up with her for a while then his mind began to wander back to the case. He wondered why Martin would try and frame someone for the murder, nothing came to mind and he knew there would be a lot of work to do tomorrow, for now though he could take a rest and he listened again to Judith's narrative.

Leonard was also home late that night after going over what they had on the murder case and wrapping up paperwork on other cases he was working on at the station. However, he went back to his empty cold house. He had got used to it now though and it didn't bother him. In some ways it was handy not to have to bother about anyone else. He could just do his own thing when and how he wanted to. Tonight he made himself a quick meal of eggs and chips and then sat listening to the radio while he did the crossword in the paper. His thoughts kept on going back to the murder and what he had to do tomorrow which he knew would keep him busy most if not all of the day. Certainly he would have to follow up on the lad Martin Baxter and he thought again about the man Martin had told about. He had seemed a strange man and Leonard could see how it could have happened as Martin had said but what he needed was some proof and that looked like being hard to get.

11.30pm Tuesday September 21st 1960

The building on the Industrial Estate was almost like home now to Josephine but all Martin could see was a cold draughty voluminous space. Josephine was pleased to be back though and switching on her torch led him to the corner she had chosen as the light was poor from the dirty windows high up on the walls. She had done the best she could with it. There was an old set of metal shelves she had pulled across the floor and placed a few feet from the corner and had secured the tarpaulin sheet between it and a hook on the wall to keep the draughts off her. In the corner she had positioned the cardboard boxes she had collected to sit and lie on and an old blanket she had found finished her hidey hole.

'Come on, sit here with me, are you hungry?' She said patting the cardboard box next to her.

Martin had to admit that he was and he sat next to her as she offered to share what she had with her, which Martin gratefully accepted. Fortunately Martin had his torch with him and used that as an extra light.

'When there is somewhere open I will buy you some things, I do actually have a little money on me.' He said rather guiltily as he told her without mentioning about the fact he had taken the twenty pound note from Nathanial's hidden money box, in fact he had not mentioned that at all. 'Pity there is no fire, it is cold in here.' He carried on with hurriedly.

'I know.' Josephine said, snuggling up to him. 'I don't have any matches and I daren't light one anyway in case someone notices but at least its dry and out of the wind.'

Martin could see the sense in that but still wished he had some matches with him. He put his arm around his new friend as they shared each other's warmth. Together they ate and drank what she had and talked on generally until she asked, 'So what do you intend to do next?'

Martin thought for a moment before answering 'I need to get into that man's house again when he is not there and find the evidence I need, then I can go to the police with it and get him arrested, hopefully before he kills anyone else.'

Josephine thought for a moment, 'You got in before but what makes you think you can get in again, and that the knife will be there or anything else you need and even then what if he has moved it how you are going to find it then? He may even just take it out with him.'

Martin was careful with his answer. Although he was getting to know Josephine he was not sure that he could trust her with the secret of Nathanial's hidey hole he had found especially as the money was there as well, 'I would hope to get in the same way as last time or find another way if the window is closed. I just need to be sure he is out, and then I can search for it. Hopefully he won't have moved it from where I found the sheaf for it and I doubt if he would carry it with him when he is not intending to use it. He must go out to shop or work or something sometimes other than killing and robbing.'

'You need a look out then?' Josephine smiled back at him.

Martin smiled back, 'Well yes, that would be useful.'

The thing was that Martin was very tired and Josephine looked beat too. 'We should get some rest.' He said, 'I can't see us getting to his house and finding him out now not after his scare. I bet he will have gone home and will lie low for a while.'

'Not for too long I hope.' Josephine said seriously.

'No, but I would say we have until tomorrow night to wait.'

'So we have the rest of tonight and all day tomorrow to waste then?'

'Well, yes I would think so.' He answered stretching out on the cardboard boxes beside Josephine.

Martin thought about going home and at what point the police would call round and thinking the risk was worth it said, 'We could go to my place and get some sleep and at least be warm. There may be some food and you could clean up, maybe I might even have some clothes you could have.'

Josephine looked at him.

'Oh, no, I don't mean anything, er. No just to sleep.' Martin hurriedly added.

'Won't your parents be in?' Josie asked cautiously.

'Maybe, but that doesn't matter, they won't disturb us or come into my room, most likely they won't even know we are there if we are quiet.'

Josephine paused for a moment, the thought of getting a wash, maybe a bath did appeal to her and a warm safe place to sleep would be good and what did she have to lose, 'So long as there's no funny business,' She said.

Martin crossed his heart, 'I swear,' He said solemnly.

Josephine smiled and said, 'Ok.'

Unfortunately Martin's home was on the other side of the park and Josephine was not keen to walk through there again so Martin took her the long way round and into his street. When they arrived at the house Martin stopped her saying, 'Be very quiet. We will go straight upstairs. I will go in first, you follow me and just make sure they don't see you, it would cause complications.'

Martin led her to the front door, which he carefully opened with his Yale key, and after a look into the hallway he beckoned Josephine inside. There were no noises from the house and Martin led her straight upstairs and into his room.

The room was bigger than she had expected with its single bed, wardrobe, chest of drawers and in one corner a small desk and chair. There was also a small armchair which she threw her rucksack onto and walked over to the window. The view was into a walled garden down a brick path onto a small lawn that needed cutting surrounded by unkempt weeded flower beds. She also had a good view into next door's garden which was just the same. Both gardens ended at a brick wall with a gate into a back alley, which must lead back around to the street.

'You take the bed, I will use my old sleeping bag on the floor,' Martin told her, dragging the bag out of his wardrobe.

Josephine lay back on the bed, pleased for the softness and comfort and put her hands behind her head. 'Have you brought girls back here before?' She asked grinning up at him.

Martin was embarrassed and blushed scarlet, his experience with girls was very little and he had never had a real girlfriend or anyone he could take home before. He kept busy with his sleeping bag and just replied, 'No, I haven't.' Which was all Josephine needed to know.

'So what do you do?' She asked.

'How do you mean?'

'I mean what friends do you have, what do you do with your time, that sort of thing?'

'Why do you want to know?'

'I'm just interested that's all. I'd like to know more about you.' Josephine rolled over onto one elbow and watched Martin finish off getting the sleeping bag ready and getting into it, fully dressed minus his shoes.

'I don't have any friends really Josephine, there are a few boys at school I know and talk to but I can't call any my friend and I don't have any girlfriends either. I just read and walk about, I like being on my own and being outside just watching the sky and the trees and all the things around us.'

'A bit of a loner then, a bit like me really although I am not so much into the nature thing and stop calling me Josephine, call me Josie, everyone else does.'

Martin smiled, 'Ok, Josie. Let's just get a bit of sleep then we can plan things out in the morning.'

Josie smiled back and snuggled under the covers before removing her shoes, jeans and jumper which she placed on top of the blankets then rolled over favouring her bandaged wrist.

* * *

Back over the other side of town Nathanial was seething. What the hell's happening to me, he thought. Everything just lately was going wrong and there seemed to be nothing he could do about it. Who was it that had caught him with the girl? How could there be men there who would see him and want to join in attacking him? It all made little sense. Although he had run off he had looked back from the gates and saw nothing, no people, no noise, nothing. It hadn't been worth going back just in case, so he had gone.

His hands touched the items he had in his pockets and thought it would be good to get rid of them now so he changed course and headed off to his fence. He knew the hour of day wouldn't matter. Jacob was always happy to receive him even in the middle of the night. In fact, he wondered if he might even prefer it.

Arriving there the shop was obviously closed and he rang the bell on the wall and waited. It took quite a few minutes for Jacob to appear in the shop in his dressing gown. Seeing Nathanial he came straight to the door and let him in looking up and down the street as he did so.

'A little late again.' Is all he said tetchily.

'Maybe it's better this way.' Nathanial replied taking the items from his pockets.

Jacob just nodded and led the way to the back of the shop, 'What have you got for me then,' He asked when they were safely out of sight behind the closed door.

Nathanial placed the gold cigarette lighter and the two silver ornaments on a table that Jacob used for such purposes.

It was quite dark in the small room with just a table lamp on for light. Jacob turned on a magnifier lamp before picking up the cigarette lighter up and studying it. He turned it over and with an eyeglass checked the markings. He hummed and ahhed then went to the silver items. After a few moments he put them down and removed his eye glass.

'Umm, not bad I suppose, not worth all that much though.' He said squinting at Nathanial.

Nathanial was used to these sort of comments and had to go through the same old wrangling procedure every time he came.

Now he just smiled and asked, 'How much?'

Jacob sucked in his breath before answering, 'I'll give you thirty pounds for the lot.'

Again Nathanial smiled, 'Come on Jacob they have to be worth more than that, that lighter has to be gold.'

Jacob picked them up again thoughtfully then said, 'Hmm, not solid, forty is the best I can do.'

Nathanial tried again to raise the price but Jacob wasn't having any of it and in the end Nathanial took the money. 'We'll meet again.' He said.

'I hope so.' Was all Jacob said as he led the way back to the front door and looked into the street in both directions before opening it.

Nathanial pocketed the notes and walked out of the shop. From here he had quite a walk back home. He was upset at losing his bag earlier at the shop with the girl. Once he got back home he settled down with a large whiskey. He decided he would rest up a day and think things through then maybe go out again tomorrow night, take a look around the Arboretum again, see who was about, but carefully. He would certainly be looking out for the girl and the lad first before looking for what was good for the taking in the area. The two young people would be his priority though. How he wished he would come up on either of them again.

8:00am Wednesday September 21st 1960

Josie was the first to wake up and she just lay there for a while listening and thinking of whether she had done the right thing coming here with Martin. He seemed safe enough and he had helped her but then others had promised to help her before and look where that had got her. Still she decided to ride it out with him and see what happened, he seemed different somehow. One thing that would be very good would be to get the knife from the man that had attacked her and have him arrested if that was possible and at the least it had been good to spend the night in a warm bed and not in the draughty warehouse.

Martin woke soon afterwards and got up immediately, 'Hi did you sleep all right?' He asked.

'Yes, thanks, what time is it?'

Martin did not have a clock in his room and he consulted his watch, 'It's a quarter past eight. My dad will either have left for work by now or he will still be asleep if he is not going out so we needn't worry about him and my mum is probably downstairs.'

'We should get going,' Josie said swinging her legs out of bed and pulling on her jeans and shoes much to Martins embarrassment and he looked away quickly, got up and put the sleeping bag away then tied his shoes on.

'We could just stay here a while longer.' He said as Josie tied up her shoe laces.

'But your mum might come up and find me.'

'That's not very likely, she never does, she may shout me though and anyway I could go down now and get us something for breakfast and bring it up.'

'Wouldn't that be a bit obvious?'

'Not if I am careful and anyway I often bring things up here to eat.'

Josie looked uncomfortable, 'Ok if you're sure. Where is the bathroom?'

'Just along the corridor, come on I will show you,' Martin led the way and showed her the room then left her, deciding to wait until she came out again to go downstairs so any sounds she may make would appear to be from him. He checked in his wardrobe making sure that his bloodied raincoat was still there and also for anything of a suitable size that he could give Josie to wear.

Josie enjoyed her time in the bathroom, she took off the bandage and examined her wrist. It was still a little swollen and ached when she moved it around but it was certainly better than it had been. She had a good wash, a bath would just be too much and take too long she decided. She washed her hair and combed it through and also had a go at trying to remove some stains from her clothes though rather ineffectually.

By the time she got back to the room Martin was getting anxious and said, 'Wait here and don't make a noise, I won't be long.' Martin left the room and closed the door before making his way downstairs after a quick trip to bathroom himself.

His mother was in the kitchen and there was a smell of burning toast. 'Do you want some?' She asked, pulling the grill pan from the gas stove.

Martin paused before saying, 'Yes, but don't worry, I will make myself some.' He checked the tea pot and found it to be hot.

'I've just brewed a pot.' His mother said brusquely.

Martin busied himself replenishing the grill pan with fresh bread and poured a large mug of tea, which he sugared, hoping that Josie liked her tea sweet.

'Did you find a job then?' She asked pouring herself another mug of tea.

Martin was caught off guard, 'Er, no, well I did look around and went asking at a few places but no one had anything to offer me.' He said shyly.

'As usual. I assume you have checked the paper and looked in at the job centre?'

'Yes, mum,' Martin sighed at her, 'I haven't been able to find anything yet but I will keep on trying, honest.'

'You better, money doesn't grow on trees you know.'

'I know. I will try again today.' Martin had nothing more to say and just hoped his mother wouldn't be long in leaving the kitchen.

Josie was beginning to fret, should she just go? She thought. Being here felt very strange now that she was alone. The house was very quiet and she didn't know if Martin was actually doing what he said he would. Was there anyone else in the house? It was all getting too much for her. Making up her mind she checked she had everything and took up her rucksack then crept quietly to the door.

By the time the toast was ready, Martin's mum had left the kitchen and taken her breakfast into the living room so she could watch the morning television at the same time. Martin quickly filled another mug of tea and piled toast up on a plate, then with the plate in one hand and two mugs in the other he made his way back upstairs. He had to put the plate down to open the door of his room and then he was inside.

He was surprised to find Josie standing in front of him all ready to go, 'Josie, what are you doing, don't go. I have breakfast for you.' Martin stood there confused and Josie immediately took pity on him and shrugged off her rucksack with a sigh of relief.

'I suddenly felt I had to go,' she said self consciously, but now you are back...' She gratefully took the offered mug of tea and a slice of buttered toast.

Together they sat on the bed and polished off all the toast and tea.

Then Martin said, 'That should keep us going for a little while.'

'So what now?'

'We go and check that mans house out.'

'Is that the right thing to do, shouldn't we wait till night again?'

'He probably won't go out again till night time if he keeps to form but then you never know, we need to be there when he does leave the house whenever he does, he may go shopping or something and anyway I want to show you his house before it gets dark again.'

'And what if he sees us?'

Martin considered this, 'He will find it hard to recognise us, I will wear different clothes anyway and maybe if you can too?'

Josie shuffled on the bed, 'I don't have much to change into.'

Martin put a hand on her shoulder, 'Never mind, it's ok, look you can wear one of my jackets, it may be a little loose but it will do.' Martin pulled a black casual coat out of his wardrobe and gave it to her, 'He won't recognise you I'm sure and anyway you can keep hidden and just keep a lookout for me, there shouldn't be any need for him to see you at all.'

'Hmm, well ok and I would like to see where he lives.' Jose said as she tried on the jacket, which fitted surprisingly well and was warm and comfortable.

'It makes sense, we will see clearer in the day and there are a couple of places we can hide in the street and garden so we will go for a look and see what we can see.'

'Is that your plan?' Josie stood with her hands on the hips.

Martin paused, 'Hmm well maybe we need to plan a bit better than that.'

Josie turned to him, 'We need a definite plan, we can't just go there and hope for the best there are too many things that could go wrong.'

Martin paused and sat on the bed. Josie sat beside him, 'So let's think it through.'

'Ok, well first we have to get there.' Martin said.

'Not so fast, can we take some supplies with us because it sounds to me that we are going to be in for a long wait and I get hungry.'

Martin had to agree with that, 'There isn't much here actually,' He said lamely having already checked while he was downstairs but being thankful for the twenty pound note he went on, 'But we can get some things from the shops while we go, I have a little money to spend.'

'Ok, fine, I can fill my bottle with water though, have you got one?'

'I can find one yes, I can see that would all be useful. When we get there we could go straight to the garden.'

'Will you be able to check if he leaves the house from there.'

'Well, no, but there is a good view into the kitchen and I saw him there last time before he went out.'

Josie was not so sure, 'Hmm, it looks like I or we will have to watch from the street to be sure. Now,' She said, 'Are you sure that he only goes out at night?'

Martin squirmed around, 'I can't be sure of that no, but so far he has yes.'

'We will have to assume that he will tonight as well then otherwise goodness knows how many days we will be out there and after a time we are bound to have people get suspicious of what we are doing but then if he does go out in the day we still need to be ready for him.' She sat thinking.

'I know, but we can try tonight anyway. I had better get changed.'

Martin got ready in different clothes while Josie turned her back and she asked, 'Are there many good places to keep watch from in the street?'

'There is an alleyway beside an empty house I used last time, no one bothered me and there is a shop, we could even watch from the street corner or there is an open area at the end of the street, so yes I suppose there are plenty of places.' Martin answered while changing into blue jeans, a green sweater and a dark brown jacket with a zip up the front.

'Well that gives us three places at least and like you said there is the garden and the alleyway too.'

'I don't think we can plan much more than that, we really will have to just see how it goes Josie.' Martin turned to look at her and was happy with the way they both looked.

Resignedly Josie had to agree with him and she stood up and shouldered her rucksack.

Martin quietly opened the door and went out onto the landing, Josie close up behind him. That was then his mum decided to go upstairs and Martin only just managed to push Josie back into his room in time before his mum was up on the landing. Closing the door on Josie Martin turned to face his mum.

'So what are you doing today?' She asked more like a statement.

'I am going again looking for a job.' Martin replied staying by the door.

His mum grunted, 'It's about time you found one you can keep, that last one didn't last long.'

'I told you why it didn't. That job was no good for me. I don't like being cooped up somewhere all day with no windows and besides they weren't doing very well and didn't really have any work for me.'

His mother stood looking at him, 'Beggars can't be choosers remember that, you need a job, and I need your board money. I haven't had any for ages.'

'I will get one mum, soon.'

His mother just grunted again and walked on to the bathroom. Martin quickly got Josie out and led her downstairs and out through the front door and into the street. Making her wait there he took her bottle to fill up with water and found one for himself as well. He worked as fast as he could then joined her again outside.

'I couldn't help but hear Martin, what are you doing about getting a job?' Josie asked staying close by his side as they walked away.

'I do need one but I can't find anything suitable. All the ones I have had so far have involved some heavy work in dirty or dark places, I just can't stand that. I need to be outside or at least in somewhere with windows.'

'I can understand that, I don't know how easy they are to get though, never having tried to get a job, though I suppose that at eighteen most people have a job or are looking for one.' Josie looked down as she walked along.

'I'm eighteen and have been working or looking for work for three years now without much success.' Martin said.

'I would have thought a person like you would get work easily enough.'

'Not so, I did reasonably well at school in some subjects but I don't have any qualifications, I failed the eleven plus and most other exams, I'm no good at that sort of thing.' Martin was frustrated with himself and the circumstances he had experienced at school.

Josie laughed, 'More a hands on kind of person are you?' They both smiled and Josie linked her arm in his as they kept walking.

In time they came to the street where Nathanial lived and Martin stopped them at the corner, 'Here it is, now we must be careful.'

'He won't be expecting a boy and a girl together though will he?' Josie said carrying on into the street and pulling Martin with her. Martin hadn't expected that and followed her round.

'Which house is it? She asked as soon as they turned the corner.

'It's on the right hand side of the street about halfway down, number twenty three.' They kept on for a few yards and came to the shop where they then crossed the road and carried on walking.

As they approached the house Josie asked, 'So where is the alleyway to the garden?' not breaking stride.

* * *

Leonard was deep in thought at his desk when David came up to him, 'Sir, we have a strange thing here.'

Leonard looked up, anything to change the mood.

David placed a bag on his desk. 'This was left at a shop burglary last night. A window was forced and some general items taken but this bag was left behind.'

Leonard stood up and looked inside it then pulled some items out. He looked back at David who carried on, 'These are items reported stolen earlier last night from a house break in. It's a bit of a mystery how they turned up where they did.'

'Now that is strange David, I supposed they have been finger printed?'

'They only have the owners prints on them sir.'

Leonard nodded, 'I see. Any other clues or information?'

David was apologetic, 'No sorry sir. Again no one saw anything but they heard noises. It sounds as though two people ran off from the scene but we only know that from the sounds heard, no visuals. We have checked for fingerprints but have only got a few smudges from the window frame where and entry was forced.'

'So this could be our long term thief or it could just be another coincidence.'

'Indeed.'

'But you say two people were heard running off?'

'So they tell us yes which doesn't sound like the usual methods of the other crimes.'

'No, it doesn't. Ok, well write it up and put it all in the report and we will see if it's useful later. Right now we have another visit to make. We need to speak to Sheila Hobbs.'

The address of Sheila Hobbs was quite close to the West's house and DCI Leonard Johnson and DS Smith arrived there at eleven am. Their knock on the door was soon answered by a stout lady.

'Mrs Hobbs?' DCI Johnson asked.

'Yes,' The woman answered already sure of who her visitors were.

Both detectives showed their warrant cards and gave their names.

'Can we come in?' Leonard asked.

Mrs Hobbs stood aside and beckoned them in, 'I imagine this is about the terrible murder of Julie West?'

'Yes it is, we have some questions to ask if you don't mind.' Leonard said.

'Not at all, anything to help, do come in. We were all very sorry to hear about poor Julie, her dad rang and told us. Sheila is really upset.' Mrs Hobbs led the way into her living room and invited them to sit down.

'I believe the party was for your daughter, Sheila Hobbs.' Leonard asked.

'Yes that's right, it was her fifteenth.'

'Is your daughter in, we would like to speak to her?'

'Actually she is, she has some friends upstairs with her in her room, friends from the party as it happens. Would you like me to call her down?'

'If you wouldn't mind, yes please and all her friends too.' Leonard said, then seeing the look on Mrs Hobbs face continued with, 'We need to find out all we can about Julie, anyone she was seeing, that sort of thing, Sheila's friends may also have known Julie and could possibly give us more information.'

Mrs Hobbs smiled, 'Of course, yes I will call them down.'

When she had left the room Leonard smiled at David, 'A bit of luck there, this will save us some time running them all down.'

It certainly will sir. I hope we learn something interesting.'

The door opened and in came three girls and two boys. Mrs Hobbs followed them in, introduced the detectives then sat in a corner armchair while the others stood in a group in front of the fire, not sure what to do. Mr Hobbs also entered and took a seat after greeting the detectives.

Leonard got all the children to sit on the floor then asked, 'Which one of you is Sheila?'

'I am,' said a pretty girl on the end of line. Her long brunette hair was tied back in a pony tail and she was wearing a flowered dress with what appeared to be a few petticoats underneath. Her round face had a questioning look as she sat with her hands in her lap a hanky scrunched up in her hands. Her eyes were red, obviously from crying.

'We need to ask you some questions about the party last night and particularly about Julie West.' Leonard started.

'Of course I will help all I can,' She turned to look at the others, 'We all will, Julie was a good friend to all of us and she was my best friend.'

'Can you give us your names?' David asked.

A bright girl with long black hair spoke first, 'I'm Susan Wilmot, a close friend of Sheila and I was also really friendly with Julie.' She added slowly.

The other girl followed with, 'Samantha Roberts, I'm just friends with everybody.' She was a thin little girl of the type that would be called a little brown mouse.

The boys began with a tall youth who was just starting to fill out with scraggy brown hair and scruffy jeans and check shirt, 'Malcolm, he said quietly as though he didn't want to give his name. David stared at him and then he added, 'Fielding.'

The other boy was plump turning to fat with a cheery face and short black hair, 'I'm Steven Browning.'

David made notes and then asked, 'What time did Julie leave the party last night?'

Sheila thought for a moment then said, 'It would be around a quarter to eight I think, I can't be quite sure though.'

One of the boys, Malcolm agreed with that time and David made a note in his book.

'What sort of a mood was she in, was she happy, did she appear worried about anything, did she appear to have something on her mind?' Leonard continued.

Again Sheila answered, 'She seemed quite happy to me, she had some new shoes and joined in with everything, but...'

Leonard took attention, 'Yes but what?'

'Well she did have something on her mind actually.' Sheila looked around again and squirmed around a little, 'She told me things in confidence inspector.'

Leonard sat back and said, 'This is a murder inquiry Miss and even if it was in confidence you really ought to share it with us now to help us catch her killer.'

Sheila regained her composure, 'She was seeing someone, someone she didn't want anyone to know about.'

'Have you any idea as to who it was?' Leonard thought that maybe he would get somewhere now.

'No, sorry she wouldn't say. I am pretty sure it was someone older than her though.' As she spoke Malcolm began to take a greater interest in what she was saying. 'She seemed excited but also a little worried, she was going to see whoever it was last night and tell him it was over, she wasn't going to see him again.' Sheila bowed her head and wiped her eyes with her hanky.

Leonard and David reeled with the information, 'And you never thought to tell us?' Leonard said his voice rising.

Tears came in Sheila's eyes, 'Well no, that is I was going to soon, only I didn't think that whoever it was she was going to see had killed her I thought it must have been someone else.'

Leonard could see the misery in her face and let it go. 'Does anyone else here have any idea as to who it might have been?'

Malcolm shifted uneasily but kept his head down and didn't speak. Everyone else just shook their heads.

'She appeared to have more money than she could have saved from her normal pocket money, can anyone give any light on how that could be?' David asked seeing the look on Mrs Hobbs face.

Malcolm spoke up, 'She seems to have had money to spend for a while. I have often seen her in new clothes and shoes and being able to do things she never used to.'

'Just how long exactly?' David asked.

Malcolm shuffled round and wished he hadn't said anything now, 'A couple of months maybe. I live close by and went to the same school as Julie and I, well we noticed that of course.' Malcolm was pleased when Sheila spoke up.

'That sounds about right, although it could have been a little longer. She would never say where she got the money from only that she had a secret little job that paid well. The whole thing about the money and whoever it was she was seeing was her little secret. She never shared it with me although we have been best friends for ever and have always told each other everything no matter how bad it was.'

Mrs Hobbs spoke up, 'That does seem strange, I know her mother reasonably well inspector and she never mentioned anything like that although I do remember Julie coming round in rather nice things. I just thought the family must have money.'

'I ask you all to think very carefully about this person and the money and if anything comes to you then you must tell us.' David made some notes in his book.

'Now,' Leonard said, 'What about boyfriends, did Julie have any?'

'She certainly hadn't had one for a while or she would have told me.' Sheila said, screwing her hanky in her hands.

'She didn't tell you about this person she was seeing though did she. Does anyone else know about any boyfriend or just boys that she might have been associating with?'

Malcolm spoke up again, 'She talked to me a few times,' He said looking at the others. They looked back at him reproachfully.

'Yes and you were too forward with her.' Another girl said.

'Really Susan, it was nothing honestly.' Malcolm blushed.

'You're just speaking up to hide what you did.'

'Wait a minute, now tell us properly, what is all this about?' Leonard asked.

Before Malcolm could speak Susan said, 'He badgered her to go out with him when it was obvious she didn't want to.'

'Is that right?'

'I fancied her yes, of course, who didn't, she was a good looking girl but I didn't badger her.'

'Yes you did,' Susan kept on, 'It's a good thing you stopped as well.'

'So did you or didn't you?' Asked David.

'I asked her out a few times that's all then when she asked me to stop I did, it was nothing more than that.'

'So you didn't go out with her then?'

'No, I never did.'

David didn't think he was telling the whole truth but there was nothing much he could about it at the moment.

'Do any of you know a Martin Baxter?' Leonard suddenly asked. From the group of blank faces and no other reactions he assumed that they did not.

'So, no boyfriends to speak of but she was seeing someone, a person no one here knows anything about and older than her is that right?'

Sheila answered, 'That's right. Julie did have the odd boyfriend of sorts occasionally but nothing serious or long lasting. There was only this person she mentioned a couple of times to me. She was all excited about him at first but then I supposed it calmed down and then she decided that enough was enough and she was going to stop seeing him. I have no idea what they did or what the attraction was, she kept that part very secret but then I did wonder if the extra money she had came from him although later of course she told me that it did.'

'Ok, well if anything else does come to mind let us know. Now I need to know your full names, what time each of you left the party where you went to and who with. David can you take over please.'

'Yes of course sir,' David got busy with his notebook again amid groans from the group while Leonard beckoned to Mrs Hobbs to follow him out of the room.

When they were in the front room where she took him he asked, 'Can you shed any other light on what you have just heard?'

Mrs Hobbs sat down in an armchair and pointed at one for Leonard then said, 'No, I'm sorry I can't. A lot of what was said was news to me. I don't get involved much with what they say and get up to so long as they behave themselves.'

'I know that Julie was best friends with Sheila and I wondered if you may have heard any scrap of information that could be useful for us in finding this person that Julie was seeing.'

'I can't think of anything, it was a big surprise to me, perhaps her mother may know more.'

Leonard didn't think so but said, 'I will certainly ask her.'

'Inspector, Sheila and Julie were the best of friends and I am surprised that she didn't say more about this person so I can only guess that it was quite a serious relationship of sorts or may be it was something more sinister, it sounds really strange. I will certainly listen out and see if I can get anything else from Sheila or those friends of hers but I fear that will be difficult. The extra money she had is a bit of a worry too isn't it?'

'Yes it is. Thank you very much Mrs Hobbs, much appreciated.' Leonard got up her and went to see how David was getting on while Mrs Hobbs followed him out.

After a few minutes David closed his notebook and got up to leave.

Leonard thanked everyone for their help and led the way out of the house. Back in the car he asked David if he had got any other useful information.

'No sir I am afraid not. The only real lead we have is on the man that Martin has reported to us and of course Martin himself and this could be the same man Julie was seeing, it all seems to match in.'

'Yes you are right, I think it's time we had another chat with the lad, Martin Baxter, see if we can get anything else from him. Lunch time should be a good time to find someone in come on lets' take a ride over there.'

* * *

When the detectives had left Sheila and her friends went back up to Sheila's bedroom. Sheila closed the door when they were all in and said, 'I wonder if they will catch him?'

Susan answered sitting on the bed with Samantha, 'I doesn't sound as though they have much to go on does it, I mean none of us know about this man she was seeing and what was that about a Martin Baxter, I've never heard of him.' The others shook their heads.

Sheila clasped her hands and said, 'I don't know a Martin Baxter but I do know that Julie was seeing someone and I don't think she really liked him that much.'

'Why do you say that?' Malcolm asked kneeling on the bed behind the girls and suddenly paying attention.

Sheila looked at him, 'Well, it's just things she said, I mean she didn't actually tell me who he was or what he looked like, in fact she never described him at all but she couldn't resist saying a few things about him when we were together.' Sheila went and sat on a small chair beside the bed.

'Oh do go on Sheila, it sounds so mysterious and fascinating, I never suspected a thing?' Susan said.

'It was like that for me too when I was asking Julie about him but she wouldn't say much only that it was quite a beneficial arrangement for her and that it wouldn't be for long.'

'But she must have said something more than that?' Malcolm added.

'Not really and that was what made it so mysterious. She would never say where they were going or what exactly they did together. She was always a little excited when they were going to meet and she made me promise not to say anything so I don't think her parents knew anything about it either. But now, now that she's gone I suppose I can tell what I know.'

'It doesn't sound like you have very much to tell to me.' Steven said. He was a quiet boy and shuffled round. He was sitting on the edge of the bed behind the girls.

'Well,' Sheila lowered her voice and leaned in closer to the others, 'She did say that he was a lot taller than her and that he always wore a hat and a overcoat so she never really got to see him but he did pay her for doing work for him although she would never say what the work was.'

Malcolm froze on hearing this and then asked, 'Did she describe him in any other way?'

'I can't think of anything Malcolm, why do you want to know?'

'Well this could be the man who killed her don't you think, after all it does seem rather odd her going off with this man that no one knows anything about.'

'It certainly does Sheila and maybe the police ought to know all this.' Susan said looking a little concerned.

Malcolm flashed a look at Susan as Sheila answered, 'I suppose they should really, do you think I should go and tell them?'

Susan was about to speak when Malcolm said, 'Maybe not yet. You don't really have any information that they can use, just a man in a hat and a coat, I doubt if that is going to be of much help.'

'Maybe so, but I just can't think of anything else she told me about him, it was such a big secret and I never thought she get hurt never mind.....' Tears came down Sheila's face and Susan quickly put an arm around her.

'Could this be connected to that thing she had with those girls from 5B?' Steven suddenly said. They all looked at him.

'That was a long while ago Samantha said. 'Julie got over all that and anyway a man wasn't involved in it.'

Sheila wiped her eyes and said, 'How Julie got involved with those terrible girls I don't know but I do know she was mortified when the shoplifting thing all came out.'

Malcolm shifted on the bed and said, 'We shouldn't talk about that, as Sam said it was a while ago now.'

'Yes but if she could do that then do you think that she may have got up to something illegal with this mystery man?' Samantha added.

'I doubt that very much Sheila, Julie was one of us, she wouldn't do anything like that again after all that trouble she got into going around with that bad lot.' Malcolm said forcibly.

Sam shook her head and kept quiet.

'Look, I think Sheila has had quite enough for tonight, I think we should all go.' Susan said getting up.

Sheila murmured a thanks and her friends all said their farewells and trooped out of the room. Malcolm left deep in thought.

* * *

Within minutes of leaving the West's Leonard Johnson and David Smith were at the Baxter's house and were ringing the doorbell. After a wait and two rings later Mrs Baxter finally opened the door.

'Yes,' She said, 'What do you want?'

'Mrs Baxter I am DCI Johnson and this is DS Smith. We need to speak to Martin Baxter, is he in?' Leonard asked as they both showed their warrant cards.

Mrs Baxter was shocked and paused for a moment before saying, 'No he's not and I don't know where he is. He sneaked out this morning with a girl that he thought I didn't know about and he didn't say where he was going.'

'He is unemployed isn't he Mrs Baxter?' David asked.

'So what of it and anyway why do you want to talk to him, it's not about that girl is it?'

Leonard and David exchanged glances before David said, 'Which girl is that Mrs Baxter?'

'Why the girl he went off with this morning of course. Thought he could pull the wool over my eyes, but he's got to be a bit sharper than that. I knew she was here all right.'

Leonard sighed, 'It's not about her no. He witnessed a murder Mrs Baxter, has he not mentioned it to you?'

'You what!'

'He reported it to us and we are now investigating and we need to speak with him again.'

Mrs Baxter looked up and down the street in case anyone had heard and Leonard asked, 'May we come in Mrs Baxter?'

'You had better, I don't want the whole street listening.' Mrs Baxter stood aside while the two men entered from the empty street.

She ushered them into the living room through a shabby hallway. The room was untidy with, items just littered everywhere. There was a battered three piece suite, a sideboard that had seen better days, a dining table behind the settee and four chairs. The table still had the remains of breakfast pots on it and most probably some of last night's dinner as well. Mrs Baxter bustled in and moved papers and clothes from the settee so the two men could sit down. Then she stood in front of the fireplace and asked, 'Well, what have you got to tell me then?'

'Is Mr Baxter in?' Leonard started.

'No, he's at work now come on out with it, what's all this about a murder?'

Leonard carried on, 'Last night your son Martin came to the station and reported a murder that he witnessed of a young girl close by here.'

'Never. I don't believe it, my Martin would never go to the police voluntarily and as for seeing a murder well....'

'I am sorry but it's true. A girl was murdered last night, which Martin did report to us and we do need to speak with him again.' David said. 'It was a Julie West, do you know her by any chance?'

'Mrs Baxter's jaw dropped open, lost for words. 'No I don't. I wish his father was here to talk to you and I am sure he will want to talk to Martin as well when he gets in.' Mrs Baxter was really put out and not at all concerned about the death of the girl.

'I am sure he will but can you give us any idea of where Martin might be right now?' Leonard asked trying not to disturb the pile of papers on the seat arm next to him.

'No I don't have a clue. He could be anywhere. He always was a difficult boy, a loner, mind you who would want to know him? He should be out looking for a job instead of gallivanting about reporting murders and going off with girls. I tell you my Jim will definitely have something to say to him when he sees him. He lost his last job and we need the money coming in. So anyway where was this murder?'

'Just a couple of streets away from here.'

'And he witnessed it, what saw the killer?'

'So he says yes.'

'Well I never. Mind you he is always out to all hours that one, could be up to anything himself.' Realising what she had just said she clammed up, worrying about what Jim would make of it all.

'Mrs Baxter, could we take a look in Martin's room please?' David asked realising he was not going to get very far with her.

'What for, you won't find anything there, apart from some dirty clothes may be?'

'We need to follow up on all we can Mrs Baxter, I have to remind you this is a murder enquiry.' Leonard said getting to his feet.

Mrs Baxter calmed down and said, 'Oh all right come on then, I suppose you must.' She led the way out of the room and up the stairs then into Martin's room, 'There you are look all you want but don't take anything mind.' She then left them and closed the door.

'Well, what do you think of her sir?' David asked.

'Not the most obliging of people and I wouldn't like to be in Martin's shoes when he returns home that's for sure.'

'Neither would I but it seems a bit strange about the girl she says he is with. It sounds as though that is not a normal thing and he certainly didn't want his mother to know about her.'

'Yes it is David, another thing we will have to check up on, it's not looking good for him. Now let's see if we can find anything useful.'

Together they searched the room looking for a diary or anything that may help them discover where he might have gone, who with and what he might be wearing. It wasn't until David looked in the wardrobe that they found anything at all though.

'Sir look at this!' David said pulling the old raincoat out. The pockets also revealed a bloody handkerchief.

Leonard took them and laid them on the bed and looked closely at the stains on them. 'Looks like blood to me, we will take these with us, go and get an evidence bag big enough from the car would you.'

David went off while Leonard considered what they had found. When David arrived back he said, 'Now why didn't he tell us about this I wonder.'

'I was thinking the same thing sir, it looks very suspicious to me.'

'Let's hope we can find him to ask him and preferably before his dad speaks to him.'

'You think he would stop him talking sir?'

'Well they don't seem very enamoured with the police now do they.'

'No indeed they don't and I have to wonder why that is as well.'

'Put out an APB and get a recent photo off Mrs Baxter, if she has one. We need to find this Martin and find out about this coat and quickly.'

They went back downstairs and David luckily managed to get a school photo of Martin that they could keep although it was quite old now him having left school three years ago.

As they were leaving Leonard said to Mrs Baxter handing her a business card, 'Let us know when and if he comes home straight away will you?'

'I'll see about that. It'll be better for him if I get to see him before his dad does and that's for his own good.'

Leonard and David had to agree with that and went back to their car.

* * *

When they arrived at the garden gate in Winston Street Martin and Josie stopped and Martin forced open the gate far enough for them both to squeeze through. Together they crept up amongst the bushes and trees until they could see into the kitchen window from a few yards away. The curtains were still open and there was no movement from inside. There was also no sign of life upstairs either although Martin now knew that Nathanial slept in the front bedroom. He was also pleased to see that the back bedroom window was still slightly ajar as he had left it.

'See the open window Josie, that's where I got in.' Martin pointed while keeping in cover under the bushes.

'That looks awfully difficult, what if the drainpipe gives way?'

Martin didn't want to think about that and just said, 'I'm sure it will be ok.'

Josie looked at him and said, 'I think this is all rather dangerous, are you sure you want to go through with it?'

'Yes definitely, I have to get him sorted out before he kills someone else, surely you can see that?'

'All right yes I suppose so,' She said thinking back to the Arboretum. 'I'll help you as best as I can.' Josie lay back contemplating what they were about to do.

Together they sat and watched for a while then Josie said, 'Didn't we ought to check on the front of the house now and then?'

'I know we said we would later but surely he would come to the kitchen before going out to get a drink or something to eat like he did before?'

'You would think so but we don't want to lose a chance with this man if he decides to go straight out.' Josie argued.

Martin turned to look at Josie, 'There is no way to the street from these gardens except through the alleyway, I suppose if we are in the street we will see him leave whatever he does first.'

'I can see that but you want to be ready to get in as soon as he leaves, right?'

'Yes, I may need all the time I can get.'

'So what if I keep an eye on the street then if I see him come out I will attract your attention.'

'How?'

Josie thought for a minute and looked around, seeing an empty can which obviously had once contained beans she said, 'I will throw this down the alley, you are bound to hear it.'

Martin thought for a moment before saying, 'No, we will keep to the plan. Now we know that the window is still open we will both go to the front and wait around there for him to come out.'

'Ok, but as soon as he is gone you hurry round but don't take too long and I will keep watch in case he comes back and if he does I will have to come round and alert you somehow. I suppose I could shout up to you or at least make a noise'

Martin agreed to this and together they slipped back out of the garden into the back alleyway and out into the street.

'Where do you want to wait?' Josie asked as they stood at the entrance to the alleyway.

'I suppose where I waited last time, over there just a few yards up and in the alley next to that empty house.'

'What if someone comes in and finds us?'

'It won't matter, we'll just walk out again and go somewhere else.'

Josie just shrugged and followed him across the road. The alleyway he had chosen gave a good view of Nathanial's house although it meant being very close to the entrance. Together they went in and Josie put her rucksack down and sat beside it on the cold ground it while Martin stood looking back at the house.

'How long do you think we'll have to wait?' Jose wanted to know.

'If he keeps to normal then probably well into tonight.'

'Can't we just come back later then?'

Martin went and sat beside her keeping to the entrance side so he could watch at the same time, 'Well we could, but like we said he may come out at any time, we don't really know and I want to be here when he does.'

'What if he just goes to the shop here and is back just as you are going in?'

'I suppose he could do, well when he comes out we will have to wait a bit, maybe follow him a few yards to make sure is going away then I will go in and you can keep watch for me.'

'I will follow him for a way while you go in for a look round,' Josie sighed, 'It's going to be a long day,' she then leant back against the wall and relaxed.

Martin checked his watch, it showed eleven thirty. Yes, he thought it is going to be a long day.

11:30am Wednesday September 21st 1960

Nathanial had been in no hurry to rise. He was still getting over the events of the previous night. That boy had been a real nuisance to him and it was strange that twice now in such a short time a boy had seen him and caused trouble. Then it occurred to him, what if it was the same person? He needed to think that through. He got dressed, shaved and went downstairs where he made himself a strong cup of tea and sat down to think.

He went through all the events in his mind from when he had been interrupted with the girl he had killed up to the present. Was it possible? The views he'd had of him seemed very similar but then how could that be? No one knew what his plans were or where he would go. The first time could just have been accidental but the second? The police would not have given his address away to anyone else, so then was the second occasion just coincidence too or had he been followed again? What was he trying to achieve? The thought made the hairs on the back of his neck bristle, if that was the case and it seemed definite that it was the same boy then he would have to take steps to avoid a third occasion at least without being prepared.

Carefully he thought through his options and decided on a few things to do which he went upstairs to carry out, breakfast would have to wait.

It was later while eating his breakfast that Nathanial thought back to the circumstances that had led to him being in this situation. He had first met the girl, Julie West some months ago. It was when he was returning from a job in town around eight o'clock in the evening when he stumbled across her. It was getting late and she really ought to have been safe at home but she had been with a youth standing outside a jewellery shop he had staked out for a couple of days and was ready to rob. The youth was a lot taller than her and he appeared to be holding her against her will and threatening her. They were obviously having an argument. Nathanial would normally never get involved with anyone in case he was remembered later but on this occasion there was a problem. With them standing outside he could not hardly break in and rob the place. He waited a while but they stayed there, then he saw the boy grab hold of the girl's arm. She squealed and was obviously in pain. Nathanial thought that was wrong and as no one else was around he decided to act and step in to sort it out. They hadn't seen him approaching but then he was so well practised at being invisible especially at night that they wouldn't have.

As he approached he could overhear their conversation. The youth obviously thought that the girl owed him something, maybe for a favour he had done. She was sure of no such thing and they were arguing about it. The argument stopped abruptly when Nathanial took hold of the youth's neck from behind in an iron grip. He struggled to no avail while the girl looked on aghast. He grabbed the boy by the collar of his jacket and spun him round forcefully. Then before the lad could get a look at his face, which was half covered by a scarf anyway, Nathanial shoved a gnarled fist under his nose.

'Whatever you are doing lad, just stop it or I will change your looks. Now get out of here and do not bother this young lady again or you will have me to answer to.' The threats that Nathanial made completely frightened the youth who then ran off as fast as he could when he was released. Nathanial then turned to the girl and asked her if she was all right.

She quickly answered, 'Yes thank you he was being a real nuisance.'

'Anyone you know?'

'Not really. I have seen him a couple of times, I knew him at school too and he, well he, he obviously likes me.'

'But you don't like him?'

'No,' She looked sheepish and Nathanial knew there was more to it than that.

'Do you want to tell me what it was all about?'

Julie hesitated, unsure what to say, 'Thank you for what you did and maybe I can do something for you in return sometime...'

'Tell me what the argument was about?' Nathanial asked firmly standing right beside her.

'Well if you must know I got in with some bad girls at school. I know I shouldn't have but I was trying to keep in with them and well, one day we all went shoplifting. Only because one girl who kind of took charge decided that we would and I couldn't back out then. I only took one small thing but he saw me and now he is threatening to tell unless I go out with him or give him some money. I would never do it again, it was horrible.'

Nathanial smile, 'Go on.'

'I did give him some money but now he wants more and I told him I wouldn't give him anything else, not that I had anything else to give him anyway and I wouldn't go out with him either.'

Nathanial smiled again, 'You did the right thing but I doubt he will come near you again. You say you would return the favour?'

'What, oh, you don't mean....'

Nathanial was shocked, "No, look all I would like is a little of your time. Just wait outside here while I go in and let me know if anyone comes along.'

'What, well I don't know, what are going to do the shop is closed.'

'It is but I am going in anyway. You just wait here and if anyone comes along just bang on the door. There will be something in it for you.'

Julie hesitated. This was obviously also a bad thing to do and had undertones of before but it was also exciting. She had never done anything bad or exciting really apart from the shoplifting episode having lived a very sheltered life so far at home and that probably was why she found these things to be exciting and different. After a little deliberation she thought, why not? A little excitement would be good and he was going to break in anyway no matter what she said or did. She nodded, 'All right then but don't be too long.'

Nathanial just smiled again and held her shoulders as though to cement her there then he was gone.

Julie waited and looked around nervously, what if someone did come along she thought as she paced up and down. She could bang on the door but what would happen if the man were caught coming out then she would be implicated in a burglary. The thoughts kept on rushing through her head and then all of a sudden he was back.

'Well done,' He said walking over to her. Here.' He said pushing a ten pound note into her hand, 'There are more of these if you want to help me again.

'I don't know, really.'

'Well please yourself but I could use you to watch out for me now and then and you never know you might enjoy it and I am sure the money would be handy.'

Julie thought that she would enjoy it, A little danger and excitement and he could obviously protect her if she needed him again and the money would certainly come in handy. Her pocket money never went very far every week.

'All right then yes I will, how will you contact me though?'

'I won't. You just be right here tomorrow night at this time and we will go to another place for you to watch out for me. After that I will let you know when and where to meet again. What's your name?'

Julie told him and was happy with the arrangement and she went off home to hide her ill-gotten gains.

Nathanial had smiled as he walked away. After all this time of working alone now he had an accomplice, someone he could also pass some blame onto if ever he was caught. It was a risk yes but then when had he never took risks, some greater than this. She didn't know his name or where he lived but he would find out where she lived.

Julie worried about her decision all night and decided not to go through with it but then she had met him the next day after all as arranged to discuss it and as events evolved she went along with it.

Nathanial then kept his agreement to pay her to keep watch for him while he committed his robberies and to help him look more innocent while walking around sizing jobs up and staking places out, he was much more inconspicuous having her with him.

As the weeks had gone by Nathanial had discovered her full name, where she lived and a lot more about her and had used her as a lookout on several burglaries. He knew she did it mostly for the adventure and he didn't care what she did with the money he gave her. He gave her a false name for himself of Albert, which she then always called him. For her part Julie was totally excited by the danger and the risks involved. She never got to see his face properly and he had told her that was for the best if ever they got caught then she couldn't identify him, which she had accepted. Being naïve and a bit of a loner she also found the contact to grow into a friendship of sorts and she was able to discuss some things with him. The boy that had troubled her for instance had approached her again but after she told Nathanial about him she never saw him again.

She never told her friends about him or what she was doing even Sheila except for snippets when she just couldn't help herself. It meant on occasions that she had to miss out on seeing friends and doing things with them but she put up with that in favour of the advantages of seeing Nathanial. She always managed to give a good excuse and sometimes pretended she was seeing Sheila. It was a little stressful but she thought it would only be for a little while.

She had thought at first that she would do one job with him but then she found that she really enjoyed it, the danger and the excitement was really good and the money was so useful. She had been able to buy things she wouldn't otherwise have been able to although she mostly had to keep them hidden from her parents. It also meant that she could treat her friends when they went out together. Her life at home had been totally sheltered and this was a real break away from it. She began to talk to him about things as she would to a friend especially when he took her out on bus trips to reconnoitre other places. However, as time had gone on and the jobs had become more serious she began to have doubts and then eventually she saw sense and wanted out.

Everything went on perfectly for just over three months. Julie had stashed away a tidy amount of money and had spent some of it on clothes and shoes which she managed to avoid her parents finding out about but she became disillusioned by it all and worried about what might happen and what her parents would think and say to her if ever she was found out. She voiced her fears to Nathanial but he always convinced her to carry on right up until that fateful night.

She had arranged to meet Nathanial that night in the alley near her home where it was quiet to tell him it was over. They had a perfect cover with her coming home from the party and Nathanial was going to arrange with her the next burglary meeting. That was until she had told him that it was over and she wasn't going to help him anymore.

The news had not gone down well with Nathanial and he was angry, after all this girl could recognise him to some extent and give evidence to incriminate him if she so wished. If anyone was going to end it was going to be him and not some slip of a girl.

He was not happy to let her go and he tried hard to persuade her to stay with him. However, she was adamant that it was over and that she was going and there was nothing he could do about it. Nathanial's anger was raised and in a fit of temper before he knew what he was doing he had taken hold of her, in response she had struggled and started to scream and he tried to gag her with her scarf but she panicked and pulled at his scarf and uncovered his face then the knife had been in his hand and it was too late he had killed her. There had been no alternative at that point she had to go, permanently.

Panicking he had taken the handbag as a motive for the crime as well as in case there was anything in it to incriminate him. It was then that he had seen the boy watching him and he had given chase. How he wished now that he had caught him, that wretched person who could now spoil everything for him. He just hoped that he would see him again tonight.

He remembered that she had told him about her best friend Sheila and what they got up to together. She had promised that she would never mention anything about him though or what they did and Nathanial had accepted that at the time. Now however, he wasn't so sure and wondered just what she might have said.

* * *

Across the street Martin and Josie took it in turns to watch the house while being close enough to chat.

'Have you really thought through what to do when you have some evidence, if of course you get any?' Jose asked.

'Only to give it to the police, get him arrested and after that I don't know, just go back to normal I suppose.'

'Normal sounds much like my normal, dismal and boring.'

Martin turned to look at her, 'Yes I suppose it is although it needn't be like that.'

Josie looked back at him, 'What do you mean?'

'We could both get jobs, lead a normal life.'

'Oh yes, like someone is going to employ me, or you.' Seeing Martin's face she quickly added, 'I didn't mean anything, you know it's just....'

'It's ok I know, we are pretty much the same there.'

'Except that you have somewhere to live.'

'That's true, but then it's not what you would want believe me.'

'So we're both screwed up in similar ways.'

'I suppose so, but I won't always be like this. I intend to do something and make some money.'

Josie smiled, 'Yes, it's just doing it though isn't it.'

Martin fell quiet and watched the street.

Then Josie asked, 'Didn't you say you had handled the knife?'

'Yes, but he handled it again after me.'

'I know but won't your finger prints still be on it, the police may think you helped him.'

Martin was shocked, 'Helped him? No of course I didn't!'

'I know that silly, but they might think otherwise.'

Martin hadn't thought of that, 'I will just have to hope his prints have covered all of mine but even so I have to through with it.'

'What if it's not that easy, the police may want to know a lot more about all this, and then you breaking into a house, they won't be happy about that. I just hope you'll be all right taking it to the police.' Josie said concerned.

Martin hoped so too and could see what Josie meant, things could be awkward for him but then it was too late now he was determined to go through with it, 'I don't have any choice now. I have told them all I know but they won't do anything. This is the only way to get him arrested.'

Josie put a hand on his arm to calm him, 'I know and I am with you honestly, all the way. I will help you all I can really.'

Martin placed a hand on hers, 'Thanks, I really appreciate it and I will protect you and once I have something you won't need to stay with me or come to the police with me.'

Josie just smiled and gave him a hug.

After an hour they both felt hungry and thirsty. Josie hadn't got anything left and Martin had not managed to bring anything with him from home, if there had been anything there to bring.

His hand went to the twenty pound note in his pocket and he said to Josie, 'Wait here, I will get us something from the shop, what would you like?'

Josie would never say no to anything and she asked for an orange drink and sandwiches, any filling would be fine.

Asking her to keep watch Martin went off and soon returned with a paper bag full of drinks, sandwiches and cakes for them both.

They enjoyed their lunch and then waited on again into the early afternoon. The clouds cleared a little and it became a bit brighter. After a while they both became restless and Martin wanted to move off but keep watch on the house. There had already been a few people notice them as they had passed the alleyway. Looking down the street he said, 'I think we should move down to the bottom of the street Josie.'

Josie got to her feet stiffly, happy to move, 'Sure, let's go, I could do with a change from being here.'

They moved off and took a careful look at the front of number twenty three as they passed. They continued on to the field at the end of the road. There was no fence and they walked straight onto the grass and up to where the canal ran from out of the town and on through the fields.

They sat on the grass and Martin wished now he had come here earlier. The clouds had thinned out and the wind had lessened making it more pleasant to be outside. There was also a good view down the road and it would be easy to see if the man left the house. Josie wandered around and sat beside the canal looking at the water and the ducks that were there. They waddled in and out of the reeds which grew along the canal edge and Josie thought what a nice place it was to be. Martin enjoyed it too and went to sit beside her but faced the street to keep an eye out. They sat there through the afternoon and into the early evening. Josie threw a few stones into the water watching the ripples they made as they chatted.

For Martin the time went by quickly enough now he had someone to talk to especially someone like Josie. He found her more and more to be really good company and he opened up to her, more than he had with anyone else for as long as he could remember and he thought that odd seeing as he had only known her for such a short time.

Josie found him to be good company too and she wanted to know more about him and she asked, 'Don't think I'm prying but just what is wrong with things at home Martin?'

Martin turned to look at her, 'Things have never been very good, ever. All my life my parents have been at each other, arguing, falling out. I grew up with it. As I got older and began to understand what was happening I tried to be a peacemaker which never really worked. If I succeeded it would only last for a short while so after a time I gave up. Dad became more and more violent too until I really couldn't even talk to him. Both mum and me had the brunt of it but mum seemed to always shrug it off and carry on which I found hard to do. I can see now that was why I never really made any friends, always being knocked down no matter what I did. What few friends I did make I could never ask them round to the house, not with all the carry on that was always happening and anyway the place was, is a tip. Neither of them seem to care what state the place is in. I keep my room clean and tidy but that is all I can do. I just keep out of the way now as best as I can and for as long as I can. I have spent most of my time alone, but I am happy with my own company. I like to be outside with no walls around me and like to see the trees and hear the birds sing. I suppose I have always had an interest in nature really.'

Josie just sat and listened and Martin carried on. 'I have had a couple of jobs, nothing special, packing, cleaning, basic go for type work, none of which have worked out. I just can't seem to hold one down for long. That's how I saw the murder, you see I keep out of the house for as long as I can and I mostly just walk the streets, sometimes until late and then passing through an alleyway, there it was and now, well I have to sort this out if I can.'

'And after that are you sure of going back home?' Josie asked softly.

'After that I don't know. I probably will go back there and face the trouble that will be waiting for me I suppose and try to find another job, what else can I do?' Martin paused and looked at Josie, ' That's enough about me, what about you, you said you had trouble with a care worker?'

Josie shuffled round so she could see Martin's face better as she talked. 'Yes I did. It was the first time I had such trouble, which is something I suppose considering how long I have been in care and around care workers. As I have told you I was made an orphan at six and although I was placed with various foster parents nobody ever adopted me. The system tried to on a few occasions but none of them lasted very long. Everyone I was placed with soon got fed up with me and I suppose I was awkward to work with. I was so frustrated and alone inside and I don't know, I just wanted to break free and get away from being told what to do all the time so I was argumentative and got into trouble, I never did what they asked and they all just sent me back after a little while.'

'What about this care worker did he bother you a lot?'

'He didn't have a chance to, I got away before it got that far but yes he did bother me quite a bit. It was at the latest place they sent me to. He seemed quite decent at first; helping me with work I was doing hoping eventually to become a care worker myself. He would come to my room after his shift and go through things with me, but after a short while his attitude changed, he would sit very close to me and make me feel uncomfortable and he would ask me about my boy friend's not that I ever really had one. The boys there would try it on, even ask me out. I went out on a few dates with one or two and others I met while living with foster parents but I never really enjoyed them. They were always trying to kiss me or get their hands on me without wanting to get to know me and I would stop seeing them, after a while I always said no. They would look at me and make comments, especially the boys in the home. I would cover up as best as I could so they would have nothing to look at which helped. I could never really have a conversation with any of them not like I am with you. But then this care worker tried to become more friendly with me and I knew what he wanted but he wasn't going to get it. I gathered from chat in the common room that I was not the only girl he had tried it on with. Then he started coming to my room more often and in the evenings. Sooner or later I knew he would want to take things further and then that night he had told me earlier that he would call and gave me a wink, which freaked me out. I mentioned all this to other care workers but they wouldn't believe me. He came round but I pretended to be ill and got rid of him. He frightened me so I put a chair under my door and prepared to go and then he came very late on and tried my door handle. That was enough for me and I was away and you pretty much know the rest.'

'That is quite a story and I am sorry you had all that trouble. What will you do when this is over?'

'I don't know, maybe things will come clear when we get that far.' Josie smiled at Martin and his heart soared making him blush. He turned away embarrassed saying, 'Yes I suppose it will.'

6.00pm Wednesday September 21st 1960

Malcolm had been thinking. He was alone in his room and his brain was in overdrive. He thought about the times he had seen Julie. Yes he liked her, more than liked her. He would have loved to have had her as a girl friend but she wasn't interested, a fact that irked him but there was very little he could do about it. He thought back to the time they had

quarrelled and the man that had come out of nowhere and scared him off
and then after that Julie must have told him that he had contacted her
again and he had caught him one night when he was going home and
threatened him again and this time he had held him by the neck until he
was spluttering for air. Could this be the man she had been seeing and
had eventually killed her.

The skimpy description Sheila had mentioned certainly fitted and the
second attack really confirmed that. Malcolm would never forget the
image of his face what little he had seen of it snarling at him as he was
held by the throat. As he went over it he became totally convinced that it
had to be him, who else could it have been? Maybe there would be
something in this for him. Yes that man had scared him and he needed
sorting out especially if he had killed the girl he had cared about. He had
to find him and confront him, threaten to turn him in to the police, yes
that would scare him all right! Then he could get some money off him.
All he had to do now was to find him, but how?

All he really knew was the location where he had first seen him and
the one where he had been attacked. He decided to start with the first
location. The second attack had been near Malcolm's home on his way
from Sheila's and that he thought was less likely a location to find him.
The best chance he had was being near his home or on a route he
frequented. He thought of the place he was attacked, it was in a back
street area away from the bright lights. Yes that is the type of area he
would frequent. All he had to do was wander around such places and he
would come across him sooner or later. He put on his black leather jacket
and left the house. There was nothing like the present.

Within a short time Malcolm was at the place of the first attack and he
looked around hoping to see him. He knew he would be able to recognise
him whatever he was wearing. The man's size and what he had seen of
his face was enough for him and if he wore the same clothes then there
would be no doubt. Evening was coming on and it was getting cold, there
was a distinct chill in the air and the wind didn't help scurrying around
the streets. Malcolm pulled his jacket closer, wrapped his arms around
him and sauntered around the area looking out all the time. He knew that
there was only a small chance of seeing him but he had to take that

chance and he wandered up and down the street and around the streets close by hoping by chance that he would be successful in seeing him. Maybe, He thought it would take several nights of looking but he was prepared to do that. The man had to pay for what he had done to Julie and to him.

* * *

Nathanial was going to hedge his bets, if someone was watching or following him then he needed to know. He had looked out of the bedroom windows several times during the day but hadn't seen anyone hanging around or looking suspicious. The only way to know for sure was to go out and check if anyone followed him.

He got dressed in the same clothes and hat so he would look just the same to anyone watching and although it was early for him to go out normally he was going to walk around and see what happened. Also there were a few groceries and items he wanted and he decided to get those at the same time from corner shops he knew to stay open longer than other shops. Being early evening any working people would be going home from work but in a little while it would be quieter and it would be easier for him to spot anyone suspicious.

Ensuring everything in the house was how he wanted it he slipped out the front door and paused a few moments, fiddling with the lock to give him time to look around. Seeing no one suspicious he started off up the street.

* * *

Martin and Josie were getting tired; they had been in sitting around waiting all day and had seen no movement at all from the house. No one had entered the alleyway either while they were there or took any notice of them where they were now, which they were pleased about but now they were getting stiff and cold and wanted something to happen at the house. Happen it did when while Josie was on watch; Nathanial came out of the house.

'He's here.' She said in a quiet excited voice, 'It has to be him.'

Martin hurriedly turned round from where he had been watching the ducks and said, 'Yes it is him, what's he doing though, he's taking a long time at the door?'

As he looked Nathanial turned towards them and Martin turned round quickly bumping into Josie, 'Quick, he mustn't see us, come on.' Grabbing Josie's rucksack and her arm he hurriedly pulled her to a group of bushes beside them and out of view from the street.

Breathlessly he waited hanging onto Josie for a minute. Josie was not keen on waiting, 'Come on let's go, he's moving.' She pulled his arm urging him to follow her.

'We have to be careful Josie,' He said now leading the way back slowly, 'We need to let him get to the end of the street before I go to the house just in case.'

Nathanial walked slowly up the street looking in all directions and especially down all the alleyways. He didn't see anyone suspicious only the odd neighbour who he ignored completely as he always had before and carried on. He walked to the corner and turned right towards the town but only went a few yards before stopping and looking in a shop window to see behind him. There was no one there. He turned and carried on glancing back whenever he could while being discrete.

Martin went to the end of the alleyway beside the house with Josie right behind him and then he glanced down the street. Apart from a couple walking down from the shop it was empty.

'You go and get in the house Martin, I will go to the end of the street and follow him a little way then come back and keep watch. If you are back out first wait for me in the alleyway.' Josie virtually pushed him into the alleyway by the house and with a backward glance Martin ran off.

Josie was not sure about Nathanial, he looked a really shifty sort of character and she didn't trust that he would stay away for long or what he might do. Making her mind up she shouldered her rucksack and took off to the end of the street. At the corner she slowed and glanced around.

Nathanial was now some way off and she felt safe to go into the main road and follow him, at least a little way she told herself. However, now she was following him she kept on, it would be good to know where he was going and if he turned to return she was sure she could always run back a lot faster than he would walk in order to warn Martin in plenty of time. She hoped that he wouldn't turn round and recognise her from the attack in the Arboretum but then it had been dark and he had caught her from behind, besides she had Martin's jacket on now and she had combed her hair differently and she was wearing a cap.

Following him was easier than she had thought; he just kept going at a reasonable pace, which suited her well. He did stop from time to time and looked in shop windows or around him at junctions but she felt safe that he didn't think anything of her especially as she kept a good distance between them. She was pleased that there were a few people around for her to blend into. People were going home from work and it was as busy as she could have hoped for.

Josie kept on walking for a little while sure of herself and that she had him in sight, but then suddenly he wasn't there. He had just vanished from view. Anxiously she hurried on thinking he must have got a long way in front of her but within a few yards she realised that she had lost him. She stopped and looked all around wondering where he had gone.

* * *

Nathanial looked around him when he could but didn't see anyone suspicious although he knew it took a little time to latch on to anyone following him. He decided to take a circuitous route through some side streets and see what happened. As he did so a group of people came out of a corner shop obscuring him from behind and within moments he was gone round the corner and then off into another side street.

There were a few places he visited regularly and quite a few more he would pass to get to other places. Tonight was one of those occasions and his route took him to where he had first met Julie West. It was just getting dark and the side street offered him some protection against being seen and the ability to know if anyone was following him. It was a little surprise that he noticed after a while that someone was behind him and stayed there no matter where he went. So, He thought, someone is following me. Now he had that information all he had to do was to lead them to a quiet place where he could catch whoever it was and find out why and who.

Malcolm couldn't believe his luck. He had only been there for a little while when who should come along but the very man he wanted to meet. There was no denying it was him, the size and the clothes gave him away easily. Malcolm was hidden in a dark doorway on the opposite side of the street and Nathanial didn't notice him as he walked by. Malcolm slid out and started to follow him trying to decide when and where to confront him. Now he was out here his plan didn't seem so good. The man was big and could easily overpower him if it came to it. He would have to start talking fast and get his message across before anything else happened. So he kept on walking looking for a likely place to talk to him.

Nathanial was a bit surprised at the clumsiness of the person behind him. Surely he would know that he had been spotted? Nathanial was also looking for a likely place to stop and have it out with whoever it was. In fact he couldn't wait to find out and he was hoping it was the boy from before although in truth he doubted it as he had been much better at this the last time.

Within a short distance he came up to a group of warehouses, trade premises that were grouped around in a yard off the main road. There were several buildings all deserted at this time of night with plenty of dark spaces between them. There was a wide entrance way into the area and it was here that Nathanial now went.

Malcolm watched the man suddenly divert into the Industrial Estate and he suspected that he was looking for somewhere to burgle or at least be up to no good and carefully he followed him in looking for a chance to catch up and talk to him. His chance came sooner than he wanted. He turned into the Industrial Estate area and realised that he could no longer see the man. He walked on a little way past the first warehouse and just as he was passing the gap in between that and the next one the man was on him and had grabbed hold of his arm and yanked him into the dark area between the buildings.

Malcolm was very surprised and yelled, 'Hey, what are you doing?'

Nathanial quickly had him pinned up against the brick wall and snarled back, 'So, what are you doing following me?'

Malcolm tried to break free of Nathanial who was holding his arms against his sides to no avail and just had to make do with getting as comfortable as he could, 'I wanted to talk to you.'

Nathanial kept a tight grip of the youth as he answered, 'Did you now? Well now's your chance.'

Malcolm suddenly felt very vulnerable and looking up into the man's face he felt the same fear he had on the night the man had frightened him off from Julie, 'I know it was you who killed Julie.' He blurted out.

Nathanial was shocked and gripped him even tighter and as he looked at him he suddenly realised who he was, 'Ah yes you were the lad I had to scare off her. You wanted her didn't you?' He didn't bother to deny what he had done, why should he? He was totally in control of the situation.

Malcolm didn't deny who he was either, frightened as he was now he had to carry on with his plan, 'She would have been better off with me than with you that's for sure. You killed her and you left her there. She was a good girl she didn't deserve to die.'

'Now what would you know about any of that eh? She wasn't that good working for me was she now for a start.'

Malcolm knew for sure now that it was all true. That the bits of information Sheila knew were all correct although neither Sheila nor any of the others had put it all together. It was only because of that chance meeting that Malcolm knew and now here he was. What was worse he now realised was that he not told anyone else. He had come out unprepared in his haste. He was the only one who knew and no one else knew he was here either. Now he had to make his point and quickly.

'You did kill though didn't you?' He said.

'What if I did? Who are you anyway? Are you in cahoots with that other lad?

Malcolm was confused, then he remembered, yes there had been talk from the police about another lad, a Martin Baxter. Maybe he could gain something from that. 'Martin Baxter, you mean?'

Nathanial paused, now at least he had the lad's name, 'You know Martin do you?'

`Yes we are mates. He knows all about it too,' as an afterthought he said, 'He knows I am here as well.'

Nathanial very much doubted it, 'Does he now, so where is he, I don't see him?'

'He's not with me but he knows I'm here and if anything happens to me he will tell.'

Nathanial thought this was quite funny, 'You mean like he did last time?'

It was now Malcolm's turn to be shocked, 'Er, well, he did and he will again.' Malcolm stuttered.

Nathanial twisted Malcolm's hands up behind his back saying, 'I don't think you know Martin. I don't think you know much at all and I don't think that anyone knows that you are here.'

Malcolm writhed around trying to ease the pain in his shoulders and arms against the pressure Nathanial was exerting, 'I do know him and he does know where I am.'

'How can he possibly know where you are and anyway, describe him to me?'

Malcolm blanched, he had no idea what he looked like at all, 'I don't have to tell you that, you don't know him.'

147

Nathanial pushed his arms up higher, 'Ah but I do young man and he does not know you are here or that you have come out here to see me. Now what was it you wanted to talk to me about?'

Malcolm straightened up as best as he could and looked Nathanial in the eye, 'I know you killed Julie and will tell the police unless.'

'Unless what.'

'Unless you pay me.'

Nathanial chuckled, 'So you want me to give you some money to keep you quiet about something you know nothing about? And you say you cared for her? You are just out for what you can get well you are not going to get anything out of me.'

'Julie told me about you.' Malcolm said trying hard to save himself now. Why had he done this? He should have gone straight to the police.

'Julie told you nothing lad.' Nathanial said, tightening his grip.

'She told Sheila and Sheila told me.' Malcolm blurted out.

Nathanial paused, yes that was possible, but then what if anything would Julie have told her? There wasn't much she could have said that would have incriminated him., but then...

'So what did she tell her then?'

'All about you, she knows everything and she told me.' Malcolm kept on willing to say anything now.

That was a mistake and Nathanial now knew it was all a sham and Malcolm knew very little at all. He did know it was him that killed Julie but that was an easy conclusion to come to after what Nathanial had done and said to him. Yes Sheila may know something and that was now something else to sort out but later. For now he had another job to do.

He spun Malcolm round and put an arm around his neck and locked his arms together and tightened his grip. Malcolm struggled against him but the man was too strong and had him in a strong strangle hold. Malcolm felt his neck constrict and it became hard to breathe, very hard. Then slowly everything went dark.

Nathanial waited until he was sure the lad was dead then he let him slip to the ground. He searched his pockets but found nothing of any use then he checked where the body lay. Yes it was in the shadows and out of the way. It would be morning before it was found he was sure. Looking carefully around the building he made his way out of the estate.

As he walked be began to think more about Julie's friend Sheila. What if Malcolm had been right and Julie had said more to her than she ought to have? He still felt safe that she couldn't have said anything that would really cause a bother but then he wasn't totally sure and he didn't want the police knocking on his door again so he changed direction and hurried on.

As it happened Sheila lived fairly nearby and it wasn't long before he was close to her house. All was dark and quiet in the street as he approached. He got to the house and checked it out. Lights were on in the downstairs and upstairs rooms and the curtains were drawn downstairs. However he could see that the upstairs curtains were open, furthermore there was a movement in the room. Holding his breath he waited and then a shape moved across the window. He couldn't believe his luck, it was her. He knew her from the time he had followed Julie to the house when he was checking up on her. Somehow he had to get to the girl. Then he bent down and pickled up a few pebbles of tarmac from the gutter. Looking around he then threw a few pieces up to the window. They clattered down and Nathanial hurried to the wall so as not to be seen from the window.

Nothing happened. He waited a little longer then threw a few more up. This time after a few moments the window opened and a voice called out.

'Who's there? Sheila called.

Nathanial held his breath.

The window closed and again Nathanial threw a few stones up.

The window opened again, 'Steven is that you? Sheila called down. Then she called, 'Look stop messing about what is going on?'

There was silence for a minute then she called, 'All right I am coming down but whatever you want it had better be good.'

Nathanial sniggered and slipped into the alleyway at the side of the house thankful that the street was empty.

Moments later the front door of the house opened and Sheila stepped out. Nathanial crept out and moved up behind the girl as she looked down the street as she said, 'Who is out here, come on out now will you, stop messing about, it's not funny now.'

Nathanial saw his chance and crept up closer to her.

Then suddenly he froze as he heard another girl's voice say, 'Hi Sheila.'

Quickly he dashed back into the alley hoping that he had not be seen in the dim light. Sheila answered with, 'Susan what are you doing here?'

'Coming to see you of course.' The girl approached and hugged her friend, 'I thought you might like some company.'

Sheila thanked her and together they went back into the house.

Nathanial sighed. Well you can't win them all, he thought and headed off. He could always come again sometime soon.

Soon he was out of the area and back on his route. Now his senses came back onto full alert as he walked on.

* * *

Josie was starting to worry. She hadn't been able to find the man again and had no idea where he now was. She hung around for a while and tried down several streets close by hoping to find him but he was nowhere to be seen. There was nothing else for it she would just have to go back to his house and wait to see if he returned, but then what if he got there first? She would have to go to the garden and somehow let Martin know what had happened just in case. So she started back stopping occasionally and looking around hoping to catch sight of him. She really felt stupid now at losing him and didn't want to go back not knowing where he was. She hung around for a few minutes at various places hoping to see him again. After a while it was obvious that was not going to happen and she started back despondently.

As luck would have it on the way back a shoelace became loose and she bent down to retighten it. At that moment Nathanial crossed the road just in front of her and when she rose she couldn't believe her eyes for there he was walking away from her. She smiled and started to follow him again.

It wasn't long before Nathanial began to have a feeling, that feeling he had when being followed. He stopped a couple of times suddenly and managed to see in the reflection of a shop window. He also couldn't believe his luck. He recognised the girl straight away and wondered how on earth she had got onto him. Then he realised that she must be with the lad, yes that must be it. All he had to do now was lead her away. He kept on walking and changed his route. Again the Arboretum seemed a good place as any to go to.

Josie kept on behind him and thought that really she ought to get in front of him to warn Martin but they were still some distance off and she decided to wait her chance to get in front without him noticing her.

As they got nearer to the town Nathanial turned off and headed in the direction of the Arboretum and Josie kept on following.

* * *

DS David Smith was feeling quite pleased with himself. The coroner's report had come in. The blood on Martin's coat matched the girl's exactly, he could now report this back to Leonard. It was just a pity they had not found the murder weapon, which meant another trip to Martin's house to try and find it. It would be interesting to see how his parents regarded that!

As well as the murder inquiry he had been kept busy following up on the spate of burglaries and muggings that had happened in and around the town. There had been a few recently and they seemed to come in waves and at random with no pattern. The evidence they had was sketchy to say the least but there was still quite a pile of paperwork to go through. The only real clue so far was a piece of cloth collected from a broken window and of course the bag of items retrieved from a shop. However, David thought that the murder had to take priority and he couldn't see how the cases were related and he hurried off to see his boss.

Leonard read the coroner's report carefully before saying, 'Yes David this definitely places Martin at the scene. It just depends now on if he was telling the truth about what happened. We certainly do need to go back to his house now and see if we can find the murder weapon and what else we can find out and we will need a warrant for that, I can't see them letting us in again without one.'

'That will take a little while sir.' David said.

'Well you had better get on it then.'

'Yes sir.' David said hurrying off.

* * *

Martin's parents were not at all happy with the events so far. When Jim had got home his wife, Mary had told him straight away of the visit from the two detectives fearful of his response.

'That useless idiot, where is he?' Jim had demanded.

'Out. He's been out all day and he's had a girl here, kept her all night in his room. I didn't realise until this morning.'

'I'll kill him, where's he gone?' Jim said running his hand over his almost bald head.

Mary hesitated, she didn't like the redness appearing in Jim's face,

All I know is that he's out.'

Jim sighed and then asked, tell me again what did these coppers say to you?'

Mary sat down thankful that the heat of the moment had passed, 'They said that Martin had reported a murder he had seen happen of a girl and they wanted to speak to him again about it.'

'Did he make a statement?'

Again Mary hesitated before answering, 'Yes they said that he has but there are more things they want to question him about.'

'The fool, I bet they have, well I have got a few questions for him as well when I see him. I have told him a thousand times never to involve the cops about anything. Only trouble can come of that. What was he doing hanging around the alleys for anyway? He's always out till late, what does he do? I tell you when I get him I will get some answers.'

Mary could see the redness coming back in Jim's face and the last thing she wanted was for him to explode. 'I don't know what he does or where he goes but I don't think he gets up to any real mischief.'

'You don't eh. It doesn't look like it. Getting involved in a murder seems like more than a little mischief to me. When are the cops coming back?'

'They didn't say, they just looked in his room and took his raincoat with them.' The words were out before she realised.

'They what! And you let them, what were you thinking of woman?' Jim had gone very red in the face and now he was right up in front of her his fists clenched.

'Jim I couldn't stop them. They wanted to look in his room for a diary or something and they just came down with it. They said there was something on it and they wanted to take it away to examine.'

Jim couldn't believe his ears. 'They found something, like what? His dinner or God knows what.'

'They thought it looked like blood.'

Jim froze and clenched and unclenched his fists, Blood! God I'll give him blood when he gets in. How the hell did he get blood on his coat, has he been fighting?'

Mary didn't know any way to tell him but to just come out with it, 'Jim they think it's the girl's blood on his coat.'

Jim sat down in a rush dazed. 'I knew it. I knew one day we would have trouble with that boy, but blood, murder. We'll have the cops all over us if it is the girl's. They will want to know everything and cause us trouble.' He sat deep in thought.

Mary also sat in thought but she couldn't say it, yes and everything you have been up to as well. The cops will enjoy all of this she was sure.

As it happened she didn't have long to wait. It was only a short while later when there was a knock on the door.

Leonard and David greeted Jim when he opened the door with a warrant to search the house.

Jim paled, then went red and angry but there was nothing he could do about it, the police were coming in. There were two uniformed officers with them and together they set about searching the house for the murder weapon. Jim was on tenterhooks watching them go through everything in the house. He tried to get in front of them in one room and remove some items but they beat him to it and he had to stand back helplessly just hoping.

After a good while David and Leonard met again in Martin's bedroom leaving the other officer's to carry on their search.

'It doesn't look like it's here sir,' David said sitting on the bed.

'No, mores' the pity. It could be anywhere, if of course he had it.'

'You still doubt him sir?'

Leonard sighed and sat with David, 'At the moment we can't rule out the fact that Martin was telling the truth all along. If the knife is not found here then we have to get the warrant for this man Nathanial and take a good look there as well.'

David nodded thoughtfully before saying, 'There are other things we have found though.'

Leonard was well aware of the items his men had found so far and that he would have to conduct an enquiry into it with all that it involved. 'Have the men list them all and check with the station for missing items and then do what you have to do then get back to the station.' Leonard got up to leave.

Jim and Mary had not been able to give any information as to Martin's whereabouts or indeed any other information. Jim had alerted Mary to say as little as possible and not to offer any extra information. They were pleased when the police had gone and then Jim searched Martin's room too in quite a rage but he didn't find anything either.

* * *

An hour later Leonard was reading through the file again at his desk of Julie West's murder when David walked up to him, 'Find anything new sir?' he asked.

'There are some things here that just don't add up.' Leonard remarked.

David sat watching waiting for his boss to carry on.

'For instance, the murder weapon, a long broad knife we are told by forensics. Where is it, and what would a youth like Martin be doing owning one anyway?'

'Maybe it was his dad's.'

'Unlikely, his dad may be many things but I just don't see him owning a knife like that, and what motive would he have anyway for killing the girl?'

David hesitated then said, 'Maybe she rejected him.'

Leonard just stared back before replying, 'Again, unlikely. They are from very different backgrounds I just can't see them getting together and then for them to meet up in the alley. It's all rather implausible. No, there is something we are missing. There is someone else involved, there has to be.'

'But the blood on Martin's coat.'

'It could be as he said, and he got it on him when trying to help.' Before David could comment Leonard went on, 'He could have hidden the coat thinking that we would come to the conclusion you just have done. 'No, we are definitely missing something here and I can't see what other explanation there can be. We could do with some proof. Come on we need to take another visit to the West's house.'

David was surprised but followed his boss out of the office.

* * *

Mrs West stood in the doorway of her daughter's room, she had been in there for hours and had cleaned it meticulously and had ensured that all Julie's things were exactly where she had left them. She looked for a few moments more, wiped a tear from her eye then silently closed the door.

When the knock came on the front door she hoped that it might be good news, the police had caught her killer and had come to tell her and that he would be locked up for good. So when she opened the door and saw DCI Leonard Johnson and DS David Smith she assumed her wish had been granted.

Having invited them in to her living room she stood with baited breath.

'Mrs West, we need to see Julie's room.' Leonard told her.

She stood still, shocked, 'But, but I thought you were going to tell me that you had caught him.' She said wringing her hands, tears starting to form again in her eyes.

'I am awfully sorry Mrs West but no, we haven't caught anyone yet that's why we need your help again.' David said.

'But you can't, I mean, I have just cleaned the room up, your other officers and yourselves have already seen the room anyway and they left it in a right state.' Mrs West was not keen on having people in there again as she wanted to keep it just as it was in memory of her daughter.

Mr West rose and put an arm around his wife's shoulders, 'They are only doing their job Jean If they want to see the room then we have to let them.'

'We do need to look again I'm afraid, you never know there may be something there we can use.'

The tears started to fall down her face and she hurried over to a corner sobbing and sank into an armchair.

'Come on I will show you up.' Mr West said leading the way. On the staircase he said, 'She had taken it very badly as indeed we all have inspectors but we will do all we can to help. She intends to keep the room exactly as it was, well for now anyway so I would appreciate it if you could cause as little disruption as possible.'

'Of course sir we will be as careful as we can be.' Leonard said.

'Are you any closer to finding who did this inspector?'

Leonard paused before answering, 'We have a couple of leads that we need to follow up on but there's nothing much else I can tell you at the minute.'

Mr West grimaced, 'And what do you think you will find in her room this time?'

'We don't know, there are some unanswered questions and I'm hoping that we may just get lucky now we have had time to delve deeper into her murder.'

At the room door Mr West stopped and said, 'Well I wish you very good luck.' before leaving them to it.

'Right David, let's get to work, look through everything, leave nothing unturned there has to be something here that can help us.' Leonard said opening the dressing table drawers, and especially look for those missing diary pages.'

6:30pm Wednesday September 21st 1960

Martin got back to the garden very quickly and went straight to the drainpipe. He tested the stability of the pipe by shaking it a little while looking up to ensure that the window was still ajar which thankfully it was. The fittings on the drainpipe had seen better days and his climbing up and down it hadn't done them any good at all but they seemed firm enough although they rattled a lot but in any case Martin was committed now, he was going to have to go up regardless.

Carefully he started to inch his way up and about halfway there was a loud creaking sound and the drainpipe suddenly moved outwards by a couple of inches. Martin froze hanging onto the pipe. Carefully he pushed down again with his feet and felt the pipe move some more. Horrified that it might give way he paused for a moment and tried to get his feet to find purchase on the bricks with little success and he had to inch very carefully up until he could get hold of the window ledge. He was then able to pull the downpipe closer to the wall with his legs and being able to hold on he pushed the window up with one hand having loosened the window before on his previous trip and eased himself thankfully through the window. As he let go of the pipe it shuddered back into position with a jangling sound and was left at a jaunty angle. He now had to hope it would be all right to go down on again once he had the evidence he wanted.

Once inside he quickly left the room he was in out onto the landing and into the front bedroom where he knew Nathanial kept the money box and sheaf stashed away. He was in the cupboard very quickly and carefully he prised the loose boards up with the penknife he had brought with him from his dad's toolbox. Then he sat back in shock, the space was empty, no knife, no money. There was nothing except a small stepladder set against the wall and a torch on a small shelf in the cupboard!

Martin didn't know what to do or think, had Nathanial took it all with him? No, he thought, that was not likely, the knife yes but all the money? He must have moved them although Martin couldn't think why or where to. Unless Nathanial was a bit paranoid about being broke into and having them stolen so maybe he hid them somewhere else from time to time. He would have to search and try to find them and quickly. He then thought about the open window, surely if Nathanial was worried about being broken into he would have made sure the windows were all closed. He ran back to the window and tried to close the open sash. He got it so far then it stuck and would not go any further. So that was why it was always open, he relaxed then thinking Nathanial just couldn't have got round to mending it or was waiting for the landlord to do it if he rented the house.

From his last search he knew the house fairly well and what places there were to hide things in but now he would have to start all over again searching. He began where he was and opened every door and drawer he could find, he looked under the carpets for any other loose boards and in every crevice he could find but there was nothing. He moved on from room to room and soon he had searched the entire upstairs. He ran downstairs conscious of how long this was taking him and wondering where Nathanial was now and what Josie was doing and how far she had followed him. He hoped she would warn him in time to get out if the man returned while he was still in the house.

The downstairs back room was obviously well lived in, there was an old three piece suite laid out with a long coffee table in front of it where there was a pile of newspapers. Sideboards ran along two walls, which had a few ornaments on and there was a large radio on a small table to the side of the fireplace. There were not really that many places to hide anything but Martin systematically went through the entire room very carefully. He stood back confident he had searched everywhere and moved on to the kitchen. This room was also well organised as it had been last time and Martin knew what was in every cupboard and where the most likely places were but although he searched very hard he did not find what he wanted. Desperately he searched the bathroom, hallways and everywhere he could think of including the toilet cistern.

With the whole house searched he didn't know now what to do or where else to look. There was just nowhere else to search. Despondently he climbed the stairs again to leave by the window. It was just so frustrating and upsetting, now he would not be able to take the knife to the police or get this terrible man arrested and although he hated himself for thinking it he now didn't know where all that money was either. Ah well, he thought, It's just too bad, I will have to go back to Josie empty handed and that man will be able to go on about his horrible business.

He wondered how she would take it, here he was trying to do good and again as usual he was a failure just like all the other times he had tried to do something no matter how small it was it never quite worked out for him. So on he went up the stairs his head low and his hand dragging on the banister.

When he reached the back bedroom he went again to the window and pulled it up as it complained loudly until the gap was big enough for him to get through. He stood there for some moments wondering, Just where had the money and knife been hidden. He had searched everywhere and it was inconceivable that he would have taken it all with him and if he had left he surely would have taken other things with him but Martin had seen his toiletries in the bathroom, the clothes in his wardrobe, personal items around that he would have taken if he wasn't going to come back. No something was wrong, he had missed something but was there time for just one more look, he decided there would have to be and take the hope of being warned if need be of the man's return.

Hurriedly he scanned around the room he was in again and took another quick look in all the places he could, looking now for more devious places like under the carpet for any loose boards. Again he was disappointed and he hurried out across the landing back into the man's bedroom. Surely they had to be hidden somewhere in here, this is where he would have hidden them if it was him so they were close to him. He began again and checked very carefully between the sheets under the bed under cupboards and everywhere he could think of. Having searched very carefully he sat on the bed dejected. All had come to nothing after all and now he must go and quickly before the man did return and catch him in the house. Slowly he got up and walked to the door and out onto the landing.

It was when he got to where the stairs joined the landing that he saw them, two tiny flakes of wood on the carpet. He bent down and picked them up. They were of old wood with bits of white paint on them and he wondered for a moment what they could be off as he hadn't seen them there before. They must have arrived recently then he turned and looking up he could see the hatch door to the loft. The wood there was old and although painted white at some time it was now yellowed with age just the same colour as the specks on the pieces of wood he was holding.

He looked more carefully and then he could also see scuff marks on the walls together with marks on the hatch door showing recent use. He looked around for something to stand on to reach the hatch door. Then he remembered and realised what the small set of steps were for in the cupboard in the front bedroom. Quickly he went and fetched them and putting them in place he climbed up and opened the loft hatch door, which dropped down on hinges away from him towards the stairs. Then he reached up and pulled himself up to take a look into the loft. There was no light so he would need a torch. Of course, he had seen one in the cupboard, so back he went and got it, it was bigger than his and would be ok to use in the dark loft.

Inside the loft the roof was quite high under the pitched roof and he was able to stand up though carefully on the beams. He shone the torch around looking for any clue as to whether the man had hidden the cash and knife up there. There wasn't much to see apart from dust, cobwebs and a few items of rubbish lying around. In certain places there was sheets that looked like sheep's wool, presumably used as insulation. As he began to scan the torch around there was no sign of anything, then as he looked closer he could see where the dust had been scuffed off certain beams and he followed the trail down into the eaves. Here he could see where the wool had been disturbed and poking around he found that underneath was what he was looking for. There was the metal box and inside was the money and the knife in its sheaf.

7:00pm Wednesday September 21st 1960

Josie was getting into the swing of following Nathanial. It was quite easy really; she just kept a good distance behind him and paused when he did. She even crossed the road a couple of times just to break it up a bit and she was quite sure that he did not suspect a thing. She began to feel quite like a spy she had seen at the pictures in some film or other following his prey. This was different of course; if he spotted her she would become his prey!

Nathanial kept on walking along. He had his hands thrust deep in his pockets and his head bowed mostly against the cold wind that gusted up now and then as he rounded the street corners. It was getting darker and there were less people about on the route he was taking. All he had to do now was keep going until he got to where he wanted to be. He thought himself to be quite clever. After all he had accomplished what he had wanted to. Now he knew who was interested in him and was following him about. He had been surprised though to discover that it was the girl he had attacked in the Arboretum. She was quite young and should not be walking around on her own as she was doing. He had noted the rucksack and the scruffy clothes too and wondered what kind of a life she was living. Obviously she was on the take for anything that she could get but then who wasn't? It was rather interesting and he couldn't wait to talk to her, on his grounds of course. On and on he walked, gradually changing course and heading more and more back towards the park. He didn't want to scare her off so he did all he could to make her feel confident and sure of not being spotted. He needed somewhere nice and quiet and the Arboretum seemed as good a place as any and that was where he headed keeping to a medium pace that she could easily keep up with but not too hurried.

Josie kept on following blissfully unaware that she had been observed. She wondered where he was going as he had not actually gone into anywhere, no shops or houses. Was he just wandering around she thought, looking for whatever or was he going to end up somewhere. She was a little surprised when he started to circle back and head out of town and even more surprised as he seemed to be heading in the direction of the Arboretum. She was also wondering how Martin had got on and if he had retrieved the knife yet? She really hoped that he had and then this episode of her life could come to an end and she could move on again, where to she had no idea, and then there was Martin, this boy she had only just met and yet had put so much faith in and was giving so much help to more than she had for anyone ever before. There was no way of knowing how things would turn out and as she had got this far already she really had to carry on and see how things ended up. In the meantime she just had to keep following Nathanial and see where he went.

The further Nathanial went the later it got which meant that everyone would be home now having their tea or getting cleaned up after their day's work. The streets were getting quieter and he knew the Arboretum would be quieter still. The children who would have been playing there will be home by now and he would have the quiet place he wanted. Just so long as the girl kept on following him. After catching her there last time he wondered if she would actually follow him in.

He approached the Arboretum from the bottom main road, which was closest to his house and he entered through the orangery. Now he had to be careful and get her to be in the right place. He went through the orangery and after a few yards he took a sharp right through some trees and risked a glance back. The girl was standing at the doorway of the orangery as though uncertain whether to enter the park or not. It would never do if she was scared off and she went out again, so to encourage her he hurried back out and walked away in clear view of the orangery almost daring her to follow him. For a while he could not check if she was following or not but after a little way he was back in amongst the trees and dodging behind a thick trunk he glanced back around it. His face screwed up into a cruel smile as he watched his prey coming towards him. He was finding this to be exciting. Always it had been him who had to follow looking for a likely spot to pounce on someone, this was the first time he had been able to guide his prey, he was getting used now to being followed.

Looking around him he thought that this would be as good place as any to pounce. There was no one about, it was quiet and there was plenty of cover here amongst the trees. All he had to do was bring her to him. He walked out again into the open and slowly walked away in a circle then he dodged behind a large bush and waited.

Josie walked on warily. She was not sure of being here in the park with a man who she knew to be a murderer and would attack her again if she messed up. Twice now she had lost him amongst the trees but every time he had appeared again. She thought about just leaving him and going back to the house but it was just too tempting to keep on and see where he went. Now he was a little way in front of her and she had to close the gap to avoid losing him. She wondered where he was going but then he had been in here the night he had attacked her so maybe it was just his usual hunting ground. Either way she couldn't lose him now. She had to keep him in sight to know when he was going to go home and maybe she could even foil another attack on someone.

Carefully she walked on looking in all directions and wishing there were other people about so that she wouldn't feel so conspicuous. She kept him in sight while staying back as far as she could but she found that now that they were in the park she had to get closer as he disappeared now and then amongst the trees and she didn't want to lose track of which way he was going. He had just vanished again and Josie hurried on knowing that he would be a distance further away so it was with a great shock when she was suddenly confronted by him as he came from behind a tree and that he grabbed hold of her shoulders.

Josie screamed and yelled at him, 'Get off me, leave me alone.'

Nathanial had quickly come out from where he had hidden and grabbed hold of her keeping her close to him as he held her in a vice like grip.

'Oh no pretty one, you have some explaining to do.' Nathanial grinned and held her tightly so she couldn't get away.

'I have got nothing to explain to you, just let me go and I won't report you.' Josie had to bluff as best as she could.

'Oh won't you now, you mean like you did last time?'

Josie paused, confused, 'What do you mean?' She tried to keep calm while looking for a chance to run.

'Don't come that with me, you know exactly what I mean, reporting me to the police, well little good that did you.'

Josie thought for a moment then realised what he meant, Martin, of course, 'Look whoever that was it wasn't me.'

Nathanial sniggered, saliva dripping down his chin, 'Be that as it may but it was you or your boyfriend Martin Baxter. You have been following me and don't try to deny it, I have been watching you. Followed me all over you have.'

Josie began to panic, how was she going to get out of this and how did he know Martin's name? 'I, I haven't I was going the same way as you.'

'Really, I don't think so.' Nathanial dragged her further away into a thicket of bushes as she shouted out in pain, 'Now we won't be seen here and if you scream I will make you wish you hadn't.

Josie began to sob, terrified of what might happen next.

'Oh it's the water works now is it. Well my girl you can cry as much as you want, it won't wash with me. Now you tell me like a good little girl why you have been following me tonight? Trying to catch me out again were you?'

Josie had to think fast. He was holding her very tight and she was so crammed in the bushes with him that escape seemed impossible, 'My friend is close by, if you don't let me go he will come and get you.'

Nathanial thought for a minute and looked at her closely, 'Yes, I see it now, it wasn't you who reported me it was your friend, a youth about your age, This Martin. Well I haven't seen him all the time you have been following me so I doubt very much if he is anywhere near here and I guess now it was him alone when he came to help you last time.'

Josie fought for time to think, 'He was with me earlier, I know he will be along very soon.'

'A lame excuse girl. Now tell me the truth, I believe you two are friends and that you two are in cahoots but where is he now?' Nathanial tightened the grip on her arms, he gripped her wrists and began to pull them up higher behind her making her wince and she tried to bend over to lessen the pain, 'We can do this the nice way or I can break both your arms, your choice.'

Josie screamed again and Nathanial took one hand away and slapped her face, 'Do that again and I will break your arms, maybe your pretty neck too.'

Josie didn't know why she said it but she did, she had to wipe that smirk off his face, 'He is in your house, he needs to get your knife and give it to the police.' It all came out in a rush and she smiled as she saw his expression change. Blurting it out gave her a rush of excitement. Nathanial hadn't bothered to cover his face properly as he was prepared to deal with her totally when he had learned everything from her.

Now though, Nathanial froze and stared at her, his mouth dropped open showing some broken yellow teeth before he said, 'Well, is he now, that is good information. Then maybe we should go and join him, come on and don't you try anything I have nothing to lose by hurting you.' He held her by his right hand and pulled her close to him and marched her out of the trees onto the grassy area of the park, 'We will keep off the paths for now, and no one will see us.' Nathanial kept his free arm around her shoulders giving her no chance to escape him.

Half stumbling, half walking Josie was forced to go with him over the grass to the southern entrance where he paused with her, 'Like I said, you come along nicely with me and you won't get hurt.' Josie winched through her tears and said nothing and allowed herself to be dragged along, thinking hard.

She wondered how Martin had got on, there had been plenty of time for him to have retrieved the knife and get out of the house. He should be waiting in the alleyway for her by now or so she hoped. After all she had not said she would continue to follow Nathanial, only just a short way to ensure he was well away from the area and Martin may have thought she had just gone which means he will have gone too. She prayed that they might bump into him on the streets or that hope on hope he will have waited to see if she returned to their meeting place and then he might be able to help her.

They didn't bump into him nor was he there at the alleyway although she took pains to glance down it. Her heart thumped and her hopes faded, he had gone and left her to her fate. What would Nathanial do with her when they got to the house and Martin was not there? All she could do was wait and hope for a chance to get away. So far there had been no one to call to on their way back, Nathanial had been very careful to avoid everyone very well. He had held her tight and there had been no way for her to escape.

'What's with the rucksack anyway. Don't tell me you are on the streets.' Nathanial asked as they carried on.

Josie didn't want to answer but said, 'It's none of your business.'

'Well I am making it my business. It seems to me you are out on the streets and probably your Martin friend too. So it looks like no one is going to miss either of you so if you want to get out of this you had better do all that I say.'

Josie was shocked, he had certainly got half of it right and she said, 'Martin does have a home and parents and they will certainly be looking for him soon.'

Nathanial grunted then said, 'Well that's as maybe but it won't save him that's for sure.'

They carried on in silence until they got to Winston Street.

At the front door of his house Nathanial stopped and pulled her close to him, 'Now just how was your friend going to get into the house?'

Josie knew there was no point lying and anyway Martin had to be long gone by now, 'There is a bedroom window ajar at the back, he will have climbed up the drainpipe.'

Nathanial sniggered again, 'Ah yes, that blasted window, I shall have to get that fixed won't I?'

Josie began to sob again, 'What are you going to do with Martin and me?'

'That's yet to be decided, but first we'd better see your if lover boy is in here hadn't we?' Nathanial took his key and opened the door before turning back to Josie, 'No screaming now, be better for it to be a surprise.'

He pushed his way in dragging Josie with him into the hallway and he closed the door quietly, locked it and pocketed the key. Josie was having palpitations and began to panic, after all Martin had told her about Nathanial, she knew that he was capable of anything and what if Martin was still here. The thought suddenly rang loud in her head. Oh God, if he was still here!

She couldn't contain herself any longer, she screamed as loud as she could, 'Martin, he is here!'

Nathanial cursed and scuffed her round her ear hard and she screamed again, then went quiet, sobbing to herself.

Nathanial, quietly said, 'It doesn't matter if he heard you, neither of you are getting away, you can be sure of that.' Nathanial threw his hat and scarf off onto a small table.

'But he could leave through the window and bring the police,' Josie argued.

'What and leave you here with me, I don't think so.' Nathanial grinned and pulled Josie further into the hallway, 'We will take a little look around and find him.' Keeping a tight hold of Josie Nathanial quickly checked the front room then all the downstairs rooms dragging her along with him.

Finding them all empty he said, 'Looks like we will find him upstairs just as you said.' Nathanial started to climb the stairs tugging Josie along with him.

8.00pm Wednesday September 21st 1960

When Leonard and David were inside Julie West's room and the door was closed David asked, 'Just what are we looking for sir?'

'Anything, there has to be something here we have missed, take a good look around and take your time I don't want to miss anything this time and especially look for the missing dairy pages.'

'But won't anything here already have been found. I mean we have already looked once and forensics have been in here too.'

'I am aware of that David, but something is eluding us I am sure of it, there has to something here we haven't found now start looking.'

David shrugged and started pulling open the drawers of the bedside table.

As David worked Leonard just sat on a small chair in a corner of the room and looked around trying to think as a young girl might think and where she would put things she wanted to keep private. He watched David work his way around the room going through her things. Julie's mother was obviously obsessed with Julie and with keeping things clean and tidy so he doubted if Julie would have put anything private within easy reach. I presume we have checked under the mattress and under the carpets David?' He asked.

David looked at him reproachingly. Then he shrugged and said, 'The mattress yes sir, the carpets, I'm not sure.' Then as Leonard kept on looking at him he sighed and looked around the carpet edge for any signs that it had been lifted. Then as Leonard watched an idea came to him.

What if Julie hadn't hidden anything at all, what if it was in plain view that would be the best place to hide something surely?

There were paintings on the walls some framed, some held on with drawing pins; all signed by Julie and most them he had to admit were pretty good. Some were of animals and there were some good landscapes too and a couple of caricatures one of which looked just like her dad. Suddenly getting an idea he walked over to a framed picture he lifted it off the wall and turning it over laid it on the bed. David looked at him bemused, he was wondering what his boss was doing letting him do all the work and now taking an interest in the pictures.

Taking a penknife from his pocket Leonard began to bend back some of the clips holding the backing board of the picture to the frame. They weren't held on very well and two of them had broken. As he began to lift the backboard up a piece of paper stuck out. Carefully he pulled it free with his fingernails. David looked up and walked over to get a better look.

'What is it sir?' He asked.

Leonard did not reply, instead he let the piece of paper fall face up onto the bed.

'The missing diary page.' David said surprised.

'One of them yes.' Leonard answered as they both started to read.

'Check out the other pictures, all of them.' Leonard placed the picture to one side and went to get another. As they worked the remaining missing diary pages were all found. They sat together on the bed reading them.

'Well I'm blowed, who would have thought it?' Leonard said quietly when he had finished reading.

'Her mum won't like to know she has been an accomplice in these crimes.'

'No, she won't and now we have a motive for her murder, just the proof we needed. She mentions money a lot and obviously has spent some but is there any left anywhere?'

Now they had something specific to look for it didn't take them long to discover a handbag that was empty but was too bulky and on closer examination they pulled open a crudely stitched lining to find a wad of notes.

'There is a few hundred quid in here sir.'

'Looks like it, don't touch it take it and have it tested for fingerprints. We certainly know a lot more about our killer now David and all thanks to Julie.'

'We certainly do sir and who would have thought the victim herself would give us so much information, so it wasn't Martin Baxter after all.

Maybe he was telling the whole truth; maybe he is involved as well. He can't be ruled out completely yet. Our next job is to find this man and quickly and it looks pointing more towards this Nathanial fellow that Martin told us about in the first place.

David agreed and taking the money together they went back downstairs with the pictures. Mrs West was not at all pleased at having the pictures removed.

'Those are my daughters inspector,' She argued, 'I don't have much left of her.'

Leonard could see the distress in her eyes and answered, 'I know that Mrs West but believe me we need to take these to continue our investigations and I promise you will get them all back just as soon as we can.'

Mrs West reluctantly had to accept that and the two men left the house.

Back at the station the two detectives had just gathered all their files of the murder and the pictures and the diary together onto Leonard's desk when an officer came in to see them.

'Sir, there was been another body found.'

Both men stopped and stared at each other, 'Who?' Is all Leonard said.

'A young man. Found just a half hour ago in an Industrial Estate off Osmaston road. Apparently one of our ladies of the night had taken a punter there and got a shock when they found him. It stopped their activities and they left but bumped into a security guard doing his rounds and they told him.

'Do we have people there?'

'On the way sir.'

'And the man and this lady?'

'Gone sir, the man wouldn't give his name or anything. He would only talk about what they had found. The guard asked them to stay but didn't manage to stop them from leaving.'

'Very well, thank you. We need to take a look. Leave all this where it is, we will check it out later.' Leonard said leaving the office.

When they arrived at the scene there were police cars there and an ambulance. The two detectives walked past the officers guarding the estate entrance and up to where lights had been set up and the medical examiner was bending over a body.

'Two in one week Alan, we can't keep having this. What can you tell us?'

'Young man around seventeen, strangled, no sign of any ligature. I would say it was done by an arm or something solid pressed against his throat. He has not been here long. In fact I would say he died within the last hour or so.'

Leonard looked up and down the narrow area. It was not often that a murdered body could be found so soon. Not that he had experienced that many murders. He stood back and looked at the scene. Why would a boy of his age be here at this time? Who would be here to kill him? Was there a connection with the murder of Julie West? So many questions, so few answers.

'Have this whole area searched, carefully for any clues David. Where is the security guard?'

An officer spoke up, 'He is just over there sir.' He pointed over to where a man in uniform was sitting on the ground with two police officers standing with him.

Leonard left David to organise a search and walked over to the guard. The man was obviously shocked and Leonard crouched down and asked him, 'I understand your situation but tell me how you found the body?'

'I was just doing my rounds like I always do and as I passed this gap I saw a man and a woman hurrying out. It was obvious what they had been up to. We get a lot of that around here, it's quiet and dark. Often they come in cars, but sometimes on foot. Anyway they pushed past me and shouted that there was a body down there. I asked them to wait and I went for a look but by the time I got back they had gone. I never thought to stop them. I just saw the body and when I turned they weren't here. Then I went and rang for you.'

'All right, I don't suppose they would have been of much help anyway but you can give the officers here a description, they may find the girl somewhere around here. Did you see anyone else on your rounds?'

The man thought for a few moments, 'No, not really, no one on the estate anyway.'

Leonard nodded, 'All right, these officers will take a full statement from you.' He then went to rejoin David.

They met near the body, 'Anything yet?' Leonard asked.

'No, nothing. Not a surprise mind you but the men will keep looking.'

'Do we have a name.'

'Actually yes we do, wait for this, his name is Malcolm Fielding. He had a student card in his pocket.'

'We know that name don't we?'

'We do indeed, he was with Julie's friends at Sheila Hobb's place. Now I think about it I recognise him.'

Leonard whistled softly, 'There is obviously a connection there. If he was killed by the same man who killed Julie then why the different method?'

David shrugged, 'Could be many reasons, maybe he just didn't have a knife with him.'

Leonard looked more closely at the body, 'Could be. Come on leave the team to it. We had better go and see his parents, see what they can tell us.'

9.30pm Wednesday September 21st 1960

Once again Leonard and David found themselves having to give terrible news to a family. Not something they wanted to do but someone had to it and they had to try and find out why Malcolm had gone to the Industrial Estate.

The Fielding's lived in a palisaded house in the same area of town as did everyone concerned with this case. Mr Fielding had let them in and they went into their sitting room where Mrs Fielding was sitting in an armchair. The house was the worst they had seen so far. They were obviously not well off, the furniture had all seen better days and it wasn't all that clean either.

It came to Leonard to impart the bad news, which he did as best as he could. The Fielding's could hardly believe their ears. They were both stunned and found it hard to find any words.

Then Mrs Fielding said, 'I can't believe it he was our world inspector, are you sure it is him?'

'I am afraid it is him yes, we will need a formal identification from yourselves, but we met him at the home of Sheila Hobbs, so I have no doubt about it.

Mrs Fielding broke down and Mr Fielding went to comfort her, as he did so Leonard said as gently as he could, 'I am awfully sorry but I have to ask you some questions, we need to catch whoever did this.'

Mr Fielding recovered first and keeping an arm around his wife as she wiped her eyes he answered, 'Yes of course, ask away.'

'Can you tell us why Malcolm may have gone to the Industrial Estate off Osmaston Road?'

Mr Fielding shook his head, 'No it beats me, but then you never really know where and what they get up to nowadays do you?'

'Was he meeting anyone in particular tonight?'

Again there was a shake of heads, 'Malcolm had a few friends but we don't ask him who he is going to meet every time he goes out.'

'You could ask Sheila Hobbs, he was often round there.' Mrs Fielding offered.

'He was, as you say round there earlier Inspector,' Mr Fielding said.

'Thank you. Did he have any enemies or people who may have wished him harm?'

They both looked at him, 'No,' Mr Fielding said, 'He was a quiet boy, never got into any trouble. He was always trying to help people. No, there were no enemies that we know of.'

David asked, 'Could we see his room?' Seeing the Fielding's looks he carried on, 'There might be something there that could help us.'

Mr Fielding detached himself from his wife who sat down and he beckoned them to follow him.

Malcolm's room was what Leonard would describe as a typical

teenage boys room. It was untidy with clothes strewn about. The bed was unmade and his belongings were scattered around.

'Well here we go again David, dig around let's see what we can find.' Leonard began by opening the wardrobe door and looking inside.

They both spent a little while searching the room for anything that could have helped them.

'No sign of a diary here.' David commented.

Leonard grinned at him, 'What from a teenage boy, not very likely.'

They carried on looking. David scanned through a school exercise book and then stopped halfway through, 'This is interesting sir.' He said looking over to his boss.

Leonard stepped over to take a look. There were some pencil drawings in it that looked remarkably like Julie West and some notes about what she had done and who she had been out with.

The two men looked at each other, 'Looks like you have found something interesting David. He obviously had a great interest in Julie, bring that with you will we have a proper look at it later.'

Downstairs Leonard thanked the Fielding's and made arrangements for them to formally identify Malcolm.

As they got in the car Leonard said, 'Let's go and have another chat with Sheila Hobbs, see if she can shed any more light on Malcolm for us.'

Mr Hobbs was surprised to have the detectives return that evening.

'Good evening sir, I wonder if your daughter is in.' Leonard asked when the door was opened.

'Yes she is, but surely you have already questioned her about poor Julie's death.'

'We have yes but now something else has happened and we need to question her again.'

Mr Hobb's wasn't sure and David continued, 'Another of her friends has just been killed and we feel that she and her friends may be able to help us piece it all together.'

Mr Hobb's was shocked and invited them in and called up to Sheila to come down. She had a friend with her, Susan Wilmot. They all went into the living room where Mrs Hobbs was also surprised to see the detectives.

Mr Hobbs beckoned the sofa and the two men sat down, Sheila sat in a chair and her friend perched on the arm. Mr Hobbs remained standing, 'Who was this other person Inspector? He asked.

Leonard started by saying to everyone, 'I am sorry to say that there has been another murder. It's someone you all knew, Malcolm Fielding.'

There was shock all round. Sheila's hand went to her mouth, 'Oh how horrible.' She said.

The other's all froze with the news, 'But he was here with us this morning.' Susan said.

Sam asked, 'How, I mean why, what happened?'

Leonard carried on, 'We are investigating but need your help . Do any of you know where Malcolm went after he was here earlier on?'

The girls looked at each other and Sheila answered, 'Well no, I mean everyone just left, that is a little later after you because we had a little chat about Julie.'

Leonard leaned forward, 'And what was that chat about?'

Sheila blushed and hesitated.

'Come on Sheila, tell the officers what you know.' Mr Hobbs said.

'We talked about what Julie had been doing and that she was seeing someone and working for him.'

'And this is the same person we discussed earlier? David said taking out his notebook.

'Yes but we don't know who it was, it was a man for sure but what work she was doing we don't know. She would only make passing comments about him.'

'Malcolm was interested in that wasn't he?' Susan said to Sheila.

'Yes he was wasn't he. He tried to get more information about him out of us but we had nothing more to tell him. It was like he knew something we didn't but he wouldn't say anything to us.'

'So you think that he knew more than you about this man.' David asked.

Both girls nodded then Sheila said, 'He seemed a little agitated and couldn't wait to go when we finished talking. I just can't believe this has happened to him?'

'I am afraid it has yes. He was found just a little while ago. I am sorry, it must be a shock for you.'

The shock was palpable on everyone. The girls all burst into tears and Sheila's parents were upset.

'But he was here with us today.' Sheila said looking around at her friend hardly believing the news.

'I am sorry but you can see now why we need to ask some questions. You were probably the last people to see him before his death.' Leonard said, 'And you have no idea where he was going or who he was going to see?'

Both girls shook their heads, 'I have no idea,' Sheila said wringing her hanky, 'I just wish we had took more notice of him now.'

'Don't distress yourself, you weren't to know and he probably wouldn't have told you anyway. I think that's all you can help us with for now although we may wish to speak with you again.' Leonard got up and

David closed his notebook.

Then Sheila said, 'She did mention that he was tall and usually wore a hat and a greatcoat of some sort but she couldn't describe what he looked like, it was as though she didn't know.

The two men exchanged glances and David made more notes then they thanked them all for their help and left.

* * *

Driving back to the station both men were quiet with their own thoughts. Together they took the pictures and items they had collected and sat at Leonard's desk, which was now getting so crowded with paperwork that they had to use the desk next to them as well.

'Well we are getting quite a bit of information now David, Lay it all out and let's see what we have got.' Leonard set to helping to sort out all the items they had.

'When it was all organised Leonard said, 'Right, let's start again from the beginning.'

He picked up a document he said, 'We start with Martin Baxter's statement. What do we make of him?'

'Well he seemed a fairly level headed sort of a lad to me sir, he seemed genuine but then he was trying to place the blame of the murder onto someone else.'

Leonard nodded, 'This man he told us about, now he seemed to be a shifty sort of character who now looks to be our man.'

'He certainly was a shifty sort yes, but then that doesn't make him a murderer.'

'No it doesn't and then there is this Malcolm Fielding. Where does he figure in all this?

'That could be just an isolated case.' David skimmed through a folder

'It could but not very likely in the face of the other facts. He obviously really liked Julie and when the talk was about what she had been doing and who she had been working for he gets all agitated and leaves then a little later winds up dead.'

'So he must have known something the others didn't.'

'Yes, something the girl's didn't all right and he probably knew where to go and who to see about it as well, how we don't know.'

'And where is Martin Baxter now I wonder?'

'That is a good question, why would he disappear when he has put this Nathanial character in the frame?

David shrugged, 'There must be a reason sir'

'Indeed there must and hopefully he will turn up soon and find out. I think we had better keep on with the APB on him and get him found.' Leonard picked up Julie's diary, 'Julie kept what she was doing from her parents but she kept notes in her diary which as we know certainly tells us a lot and Martin is not mentioned anywhere which kind of confirms his story somewhat. She was working as a lookout, and accomplice to the burglary crimes we have been having and getting well paid for it, which puts Martin out of the frame, unless he is in on it too which is becoming more doubtful as we go on. And we have these pictures of Julie's.'

'The burglaries and muggings have been a problem for a while now and we know very little about the perpetrator, except for a piece of cloth which could be from a greatcoat as Sheila has told us. It certainly makes you wonder if it is this same man that Julie was involved with.'

'It certainly does, so what does that all tell us?' Leonard asked.

David was sitting back looking at one of the paintings, it was a rather clever caricature of a man. Then he sat forward in his seat, 'Sir, who does that picture remind you of?'

Leonard looked at the painting. The features had been exaggerated but there was no mistaking that it was a man and he was wearing a long black coat and a trilby hat.

'Well I never, yes we have had a description of that man before haven't we David.' He picked up the piece of cloth in its evidence bag. 'This cloth certainly fits with the description and on that picture. That has to be our man, everything fits. It looks like we can solve two murders and the burglary crimes all at the same time. I think it's well time we paid him another call I think we have all the proof we need now, and organise some back up this time.'

10:30pm Wednesday September 21st 1960

Martin looked again at the piles of money rubber banded in bundles and wondered just how much there was, there must be thousands he judged and he wondered why Nathanial hadn't just used it to make his life better but then he thought no, Nathanial was a dirty piece of work who did what he did for pleasure as much as anything else and he would keep on doing it until he was caught or until he was too old to carry on his lifestyle. Well now he was going to get caught Martin thought as he took the knife carefully only touching the blade and slipped it into his coat pocket. Now I have proof, proof to get you put away forever, Martin thought smiling as he thought of what his face would look like when the police arrived to arrest him.

He put the money back where it was after wrestling with his conscience. It was a lot and he could make a new life with it but then could he live with money obtained in such a way, he would have to think about that one? He was edging his way back to the loft door when he heard Josie's pitiful cry. He froze. All his resolve melted away. His legs turned to rubber and he suddenly felt very hot and his mouth went very dry. Somehow the man had gotten hold of Josie and he was here with her now. He cursed himself, how could he have been so foolish to let her go after him and taken so long with his search? Now he was trapped in the house with a maniac who had hold of the only girl he had ever met he could talk to and liked to be with. What was he to do now?

Martin knew he had no choice, he had to carry on making his way back to the loft door and see what he could do if anything. He was certainly trapped if he stayed where he was that was for sure, the man would be certain to find him especially as the loft door was hanging open.

At the loft door Martin knelt down and looked through the open hatch down the staircase. There at the bottom was Nathanial and he had Josie in a strong hold struggling with her in the hall and then they disappeared into the front room. Without thinking Martin reached down and took hold of the stepladder and pulled it up into the loft and laid it to one side as quietly as he could. Then he grabbed the hatch door and pulled it up carefully, leaving only a small space that he could see through and he prayed that the man hadn't seen him do it.

As it happened, he hadn't been seen, so keen was Nathanial on subduing Josie who having seen the open hatch door and Martin's hand reach down for the ladder had been desperate to avert the man's attention and she had pulled back sharply making Nathanial so cross that he hit her again and twisted her wrist as he dragged her along after him. She didn't feel the pain, as she was so very pleased to know that Martin was in fact here in the house and he hadn't deserted her after all while at the same time very worried as to how they were going to get out of this mess.

Martin could hardly breath, his chest was tight and he was sweating, worried for Josie and indeed for himself. His mind was working overtime. There was little he could up here but he couldn't get down without alerting the man. As it happened he didn't have much time to think about it because the man suddenly appeared at the bottom of the stairs with Josie and started his way up.

Nathanial continued up the stairs, struggling to contain Josie and keep her with him on the narrow staircase. They climbed up step by step and Josie was fearful of what was going to happen next. She now knew that Martin was in the loft, why he was still here after all this time she didn't know but he was here. Was he going to get caught as well or was he going to be able to do something to help them? All she could do was go up the stairs and hope for the best being prepared for any chance for escape that presented itself.

Nathanial climbed up slowly, listening and grinning all the time until he got to the landing and pulled Josie up behind him as she held back and she stopped two steps from the top. He stopped there deciding which bedroom to go to first. It was very quiet and he wasn't even sure that the lad was still here; surely he would have made a noise by now.

Martin now saw his chance. He was thankful that Josie was on a step below the landing and so lower down than the man. He took hold of the hatch door in both hands and holding his breath hurled it open. It swung down very fast and caught the man on his shoulder with a mighty whack. Martin was amazed that it hadn't hit his head but at the last moment the man had seen it coming and had moved his head far enough just to sustain a heavy blow on his shoulder instead which knocked him over backwards and into Josie who stopped him from falling down the stairs. She was however pushed a few steps down and she struggled to keep her balance by grabbing hold of the banister.

Nathanial cried out in pain as he slipped down a few steps and clutched at his shoulder as he struggled to regain his balance. Josie climbed down a few more steps to keep away from him and stood there paralysed with fear and shock and could only watch as Martin dropped down from the loft onto the landing her throat too dry to call out.

Suddenly finding her courage she shouted, 'Martin, get away, run now, quick!'

Martin didn't have any choice in what to do as Nathanial was recovering and lunging out for him, 'Come here you, I will teach you to mess with me.' He snarled.

Martin only narrowly avoided being caught and kicked out at the man but he only managed to land a glancing blow to his arm. Then he moved quickly towards the bedroom with the open window while calling out to Josie, 'You run, get out.'

'I can't, the door's locked,' She shouted back exasperated not knowing what to do.

Martin was shocked; if he ran to the window and managed to escape

Jose would be trapped inside with the monster of a man. Again he didn't have time to think any further as the man was up and after him.

Martin ducked into the bedroom and as the man came in after him he slammed the door hard into his injured shoulder. Nathanial howled with pain and Martin held the door as long as he could. Nathanial was injured and stumbled but still he came on and using his bulk forced his way into the room flinging the door open with his good arm. Martin could see that his whole shoulder was hanging at a strange angle and must be broken yet still the man came on towards him, rage showing in his face.

It was fortunate that the room had only a little amount of furniture in it, which gave Martin some space in which to manoeuvre. He was young, supple and quick whereas Nathanial was a lot older, slower and he had to favour his injured shoulder.

Now they were both together in the bedroom and again Martin considered going out the window knowing that his adversary wouldn't be able to follow him but with Josie trapped that was not possible for him, he had to stay and see it through somehow.

Martin easily dodged Nathanial's first lunge at him and managed to return a punch to his kidneys. They circled each other looking for a chance then Nathanial lunged again and managed to punch Martin in the chest, the blow knocked the breath out of him and Nathanial came on again grinning. Martin crouched and waited then as the man got close to him he ducked to one side kicking out as he did so. His shoe connected with Nathanial's shin and again he howled in pain. Careful now he circled around sizing up what to do next. Martin waited breathing hard. His adrenalin was up and though he had hardly had a fight in his life he was now prepared to fight as hard as he could and to hell with the Queensbury rules.

They circled round the room throwing punches and kicks at each other some landing and some not. Martin hoped that Josie had found a way out, as he wasn't sure he was going to win this fight and he had hadn't got the time to relax his attention to call out to her. He moved again as Nathanial came at him and managed two good thumps to his body. Backing off Nathanial grinned again then he launched himself forwards and caught hold of Martin's left arm and swung him round hard so that he was propelled into the wall. The crunch came keen and drove the wind out of him. Martin managed to turn round but before he could recover Nathanial was on him, pushing him up against the wall, holding him with one hand and bringing his knee up hard into Martin's groin. Martin groaned and twisted away in pain. Then in anger he faced back up to Nathanial and began punching him for all he was worth. Nathanial's left arm was useless and hung limply beside him but even with one arm he was able to block most of Martin's blows and give a few blows back his body holding Martin against the wall.

Keeping Martin close to him he said, 'You are not going to give me any more trouble now young man, because you are going down. I am going to teach you not to meddle in other people's affairs. You are going to be sorry you ever saw me and that slip of a girl you have with you, well I will see to her just as soon as I have finished with you.'

'You leave Josie out of this just let her go she doesn't know anything.' Martin said in between blows and trying to get his breath.

'Oh I am sure she knows plenty, you two have been in cahoots long enough, no she will get hers soon and I will enjoy doing it.' Nathanial taunted.

'You swine, you can't hurt her.' Martin blurted out in anger and pushed hard against Nathanial. The surprise and determination Martin used worked and they separated.

Martin launched himself at him, punching and kicking for all he was worth. Nathanial took a few blows then reached out with his good arm. Nathanial was bigger and heavier and he pulled Martin towards him then hooked an ankle behind Martin's leading foot and pushed against him making him loose his balance and he fell heavily to the floor and then Nathanial started kicking him.

'So, think you can take me do you? Well how about this?' Nathanial shouted as he drove a boot into Martin's stomach. Martin tried to dodge the blows and move out of the way but it was impossible as he was unable to get up under the relentless kicking he was getting as Nathanial moved round and round him.

Martin pulled his knees up and tucked his hands into a foetal position and it was then he felt the hard metal digging into him. Instinctively he reached into his pocket and drew out the knife, which he grasped tightly in his right hand.

Josie was beside herself. The initial shock was wearing off and she shrugged off her rucksack and let it fall to the bottom of the stairs. Then she cautiously climbed to the top of the stairs again. She could hear the sounds of fighting coming from the bedroom and she desperately hoped that Martin was all right. However, the sounds grew worse and she heard the man shout followed by the grunts and groans together with the sounds of the kicks. She wanted to help, she had to help. Martin was in real trouble and if the man kept on kicking him it would soon all be over for him and for her. She drove the thought from her mind and quietly she edged to the room and stepped into the doorway. The scene horrified her. Martin was on the floor and Nathanial had his back to her kicking him.

Quickly she looked around the room and not seeing what she wanted she ran out to the front bedroom. Here on a low cupboard was a large pot jug and bowl. Grabbing the jug she ran back and entered the other bedroom. The man's back was still towards her while Martin was lying still, not moving. The man was still kicking him and he hadn't noticed her. With no other thought and her adrenalin running she crept up quickly behind him and crashed the jug hard onto the man's head.

Nathanial collapsed and fell to the floor. As he did so Martin had just got the knife free of his pocket and was holding it up as Nathanial fell. He landed straight on the knife which punched straight through his clothing, sliced neatly between his ribs and went right into his heart killing him instantly and he lay still, his body half over Martin.

Josie screamed and dragged at Nathanial's body trying to pull him off. Martin pushed too and together they managed to roll him off. He fell onto his back and they could see the knife handle protruding from his chest as blood oozed out. Josie screamed again and put her hands to her mouth. Martin struggled free and painfully rose to a sitting position against the wall breathing hard with Nathanial's blood on his hand and his clothes.

'Is he dead?' Josie asked shaking uncontrollably.

Martin looked again carefully and he was as certain as he could be, 'Yes, he must be.'

'Oh God, what have we done?'

Martin beckoned to her and she knelt down beside him and went into his arms.

Martin hugged her as she sobbed, 'We've killed him.'

'It was him or us. He was an evil man Josie and we didn't mean to kill him, it was an accident.'

'But you had the knife.'

'To defend myself with, if you had been a bit later I wouldn't have been able to use it. I had no idea what was going to happen.' Martin groaned again and tried to get comfortable his bruises aching badly.

Josie pulled herself away, 'Are you all right?' She asked, concern all over her face.

'I think so,' Martin rubbed at his aches over himself and edged further away from Nathanial's body.

'We ought to leave, quickly,' Josie said while standing up.

'And do what?' Martin demanded to know.

'Go to the police.'

Martin stared at her for a few moments.

'Oh,' She said, 'Your finger prints are on the knife.'

'And the knife's in his chest. Even if we get his prints back on it how will we explain his death.'

Josie thought for a moment, 'I suppose we could just tell the truth.' She looked down at the body, 'We have killed him and we don't even know his name.'

Martin staggered to his feet and was glad to realise that nothing was broken and apart from quite a few bad bruises he was ok, 'We could do that, if they believe us.' Martin's brain was working overtime, yes they could go to the police but that still spelled lots of trouble for both of them and Josie would be sent back into care and he wondered how his parents would take the news, not at all well he knew. On the other hand there was an awful lot of money up in the loft, enough to give them both a good start and more somewhere else, anywhere else and the man wouldn't need it now. On the other hand with the money and knife sheath, which only had the man's fingerprints on maybe the police would believe them. It was a hard choice.

He looked at Josie, she was scared and without him she would be back on her own again with no one to help her, what would become of her? Then he took her by the shoulders, 'There is something I need to get then we will go downstairs and talk away from him.'

He led her back to the landing and made her wait still shaking after he got her to give him a leg up while he climbed back into the loft.

Minutes later Martin was back carrying a paper bag he had found in the loft with something inside it.

'Come on let's get downstairs'. They went down and Martin sat Josie down in a chair in the kitchen and began to explain their options to her while he tried to wash the blood off his hands and his clothes.

Josie was so shaken up that Martin could see that he wasn't going to get through to her. That's when they heard a banging on the door and someone calling, 'Police, open up.'

Josie panicked, stood up and started crying, 'They're here, the police, what do we do?'

Martin was amazed that he could think clearly with everything that was happening. How did they know? Had someone heard the noise they had made and called them? He had no time to think about it, 'Come on I know what to do.' He pulled Josie's arm and led her into the hall. Here he picked up her rucksack, crammed the paper bag into it which luckily now had space enough for it and began to pull her up the stairs fastening the rucksack straps as he went.

'Where are we going?' Josie cried through her tears.

'The upstairs room, we can get out through the window, it's our only chance everywhere is locked up down here.'

Josie then realised what this meant, 'You expect me to climb through that window and down the drain pipe?' She asked incredulously.

'The only other way is through the front door if I get his key and the police are there so yes, I will help you, come on we must hurry.'

'But it means going past him again.'

'He can't hurt you now come on.' Martin tugged at her harder urging her on.

Together they continued up the stairs while they heard the cries from the police outside.

'They will force the door open,' Josie said.

'Yes they will that's why we must hurry.

He kept on pulling and urging her until they reached the back bedroom. As they entered Josie baulked again and pulled free of him.

'I can't, I can't go in there I'm sorry you will have to go alone.'

'Josie you must, for both our sakes, you don't have to look. Close your eyes and I will guide you past him.'

Sobbing she clung onto him and he slowly managed to get her into the room and to the window.

Looking out he could see that the drainpipe was at an angle from the wall and had slipped some way from the window.

'Just stand there Josie I need to get the pipe for us.' He left her standing by the window and climbed halfway out and reached over for the drainpipe. He couldn't reach it. Damn he thought, why did everything always have to go wrong for him?

He just couldn't reach the pipe and it was too far for them to jump without a serious risk of injuring themselves.

Then he had a thought, 'Josie,' He said jumping back into the room with her, 'I need you to help me. Just hold onto my belt while I reach out for the pipe.'

'It's no use Martin, I can't do it.' Josie was struggling with the shock and stress of the situation.

'You must Josie.' Martin carefully guided her to the window and climbed out again and gave her a hand, 'Hold onto me Josie, hold tight, then I can reach it.'

Josie took his belt in both her hands and held on as Martin stretched out as far as he could. His fingers brushed the pipe and it swung away from him. That was it, it was over, he couldn't reach it now. Soon the police would be in and he would have a lot of explaining to do.

The drainpipe swung around on its fastenings and it came around and banged into the window sill just inches away. Martin couldn't believe his luck. Reaching out he got hold of the pipe with one hand. Come on Josie, now you can climb down.'

Josie looked out of the window, 'I can't really I can't.'

Martin was getting worried, 'It's easy; I will guide you down and tell you what to do all the way. I can't go with you the pipe won't hold both of us at once.' He looked at her worried face imploringly.

They heard a crash downstairs and Martin started, 'Please hurry Josie.'

Pulling herself together Josie climbed out onto the window sill as Martin held her. He guided her onto the window sill and her hands onto the pipe but then she pulled her left hand off the pipe crying, 'Oh my wrist, it won't hold me.'

Martin glanced behind wondering how long they had, Josie please you must bear the pain, it's the only way out of here.'

Tentatively she took hold again, swung out of the window and grimacing started to make her way down scrabbling with her feet as Martin told her where to put each foot and hand hold. The drainpipe squealed in protest and Martin wondered if the police had got in and if they could hear the noise?

Eventually Josie reached the ground and Martin threw down her rucksack then quickly began climbing down after her. Halfway down the drainpipe squealed in protest again and another bracket suddenly pinged off and flew into the garden. Josie also squealed as Martin was left holding onto the pipe as it curved away from the wall. This time it was not going back. The metal had taken enough and the pipe gradually bent over until it broke.

Martin lost his grip and fell the rest of the way. Luckily it was not too far and apart from banging his ankle on the brick path he was all right.

Josie helped him up having already put her rucksack on her back. Martin hobbled along saying, 'Come on we must hurry before the police find us.'

Josie held an arm and helped him down the garden path to the back gate. Martin was walking a little bit better by then and he pulled open the gate and hurriedly got them both through before closing the gate again as best as he could and they started for the alleyway.

'We can't go down the alleyway Martin, the police will see us come out.' Josie said as they started off.

'I know.' Martin stopped and thought for a moment, 'You are right will have to try the other way hopefully we will find another way out.'

He bundled her back to the gate and started off in the other direction. He had not been this way before as there was a gate blocking the path a few yards further on, he could only hope they could get past it. At the gate they stopped, aware that they were in full view of anyone entering the alleyway. The gate was quite high, solid and it was locked.

* * *

Leonard was not going to wait long at the door and after a couple of minutes and several loud knocks he ordered his men to break in. It was only a few seconds job with a heavy hammer an officer wielded and then they were inside.

Leonard and David were the first in followed by their uniformed officers. 'Search everywhere,' he called to his men as he began searching the downstairs rooms.

David raced upstairs with two constables while Leonard checked downstairs with one other constable. It was only a minute later that David called down, 'Sir, up here!'

When Leonard arrived at the upstairs room David and the constables had moved out onto the landing not wanting to contaminate the scene. Leonard carefully walked in and took a good look around before walking over to where Nathanial lay. David came up behind him.

'Is he dead sir?' He asked.

Leonard checked for a pulse but it was fairly obvious of the answer, 'He's dead all right, you had better call it in, get forensics out here.'

David urged an officer to go and do it and watched his boss. Leonard saw the knife and guessed that it would be proved to be the weapon used to kill Julie West. He pointed it out to David. Who would have done this? There were not many suspects that came to mind, only one in particular, but under what circumstances he wondered?

David glanced down thoughtfully, 'I think we have a good idea sir.' He said.

Leonard wandered over to the open window and peered out and taking in the scene he leaned back and under his breath he said, 'I wonder?'

* * *

Martin looked up at the gate. It was at least seven feet high and was obviously made to keep people out. Josie looked on apprehensively.

'Josie can you give me a leg up?'

Josie interlocked the fingers of her hand favouring her left and waited while Martin placed a foot in them and grimacing with the pain Martin launched himself up and grabbed hold of the top of the gate, then with Josie's help he scrambled up onto the top and sat there. He looked down and saw that the gate was secured with a strong padlock and there was no way he was going to open the gate. Leaning over he held an arm down to Josie he said, 'Pass me your rucksack then give me your hand, you are going to have to climb over.'

Josie was not happy but she handed over the rucksack nevertheless and then took hold of his hand. Martin pulled for all he was worth and Josie finally scrambled up to the top of the gate and sat there with her legs dangling over the far side. Martin then took her hand and helped her drop to the ground then he jumped down to join her.

They were now in a garden that was well kept with lawns and flowerbeds. Carefully they crossed the garden to another gate, which again they had to climb over all the time hoping that no one in any of the houses would see them.

'Come on, hurry, we must get away from here,' Martin said grabbing Josie's hand and leading her on up the alleyway which now continued on.

For some yards they hurried on before they came to the end where there was a ninety degree turn to the right. They hurried round and found that the path led to another alleyway between the houses and out onto the street. They hurried along it until they reached the end then Martin risked a glance around the corner and down the street. He could see two police cars parked outside number twenty three and two constables standing outside. Motioning to Josie they both left the alleyway into the street. Here they slowed down and walked purposefully arm in arm. Martin however could not resist a glance back down the street and saw the constables had not taken any notice of them. Seconds later they turned the corner and out onto the main road.

* * *

Leonard and David stayed at the scene until forensics in the form of Dr Ian Price arrived.

'You're doing well Leonard, three in a week.' Ian said brusquely as he put his bag down and leant over the body.

'Get any fingerprints you can Alan and let me know the results will you.' Leonard asked ignoring the comment. He then guided David downstairs and out of the house.

'You think this Martin Baxter is involved in all this then sir, could he have killed this man?' David asked.

'That's a good question, what do you think David? The fingerprints should tell us all we need to know. In the meantime just where do you think the lad is now?'

Printed in Great Britain
by Amazon

83269780R00113